FYN CARTER AND THE AGENTS OF EROMLOS

FYN CARTER
AND THE AGENTS OF EROMLOS

IAN HUNTER

Fyn Carter and the Agents of Eromlos
An original concept by author Ian Hunter
© Ian Hunter, 2024

Cover illustration by Ian Hunter
© Ian Hunter, 2024

The right of Ian Hunter to be identified as the author and illustrator of this work has been asserted.

This is a work of fiction. Names, characters, places, incidents, and dialogues are the product of the author's imagination or are used fictitiously. Any resemblance to actual people, living or dead, events, or locales is entirely coincidental.

First Edition May 2024.

ISBN-13: 978-1-7385069-0-3

www.ianhuntercreates.com

For Ian L, who encourages me with a heart that contains the strength of superheroes and the wisdom of wizards.

For Delsia, who encouraged me when words were taking shape in the heart of my childhood.

CHAPTER ONE

The Unexpected Message

Have you ever heard a voice inside telling you to wake up right now because if you don't you will regret it?

Fyn Carter woke abruptly to a loud crash of thunder and nearly fell off the sofa where he had comfortably drifted to sleep.

It was completely dark, apart from the small red light on the telly and a faint glow on the walls and furniture from a streetlight outside. As he gathered his wits he glanced at the clock and was surprised to see the time was just after 2 a.m.

The last thing he remembered was watching a wildlife documentary and feeling particularly relaxed as a pod of dolphins played with a clump of seaweed. The weather at the time had been fine, but now rain was hitting the windows hard, and wind howled and swooshed around the outside of the house.

As he crossed the living room to the open curtains, he wondered why his mum hadn't woken him.

Lightning flashed across the sky as he spotted the wheelie bin had blown over on the drive, but where was his mum's car? Starting to worry that she hadn't made it home, he closed the curtains and moved into the hallway where the answer machine beeped at him. He pressed the machine button and was relieved to hear her voice.

'Hi, Fyn. I hope you're okay. I'm so sorry but the storm has uprooted a tree through Florence Park, and I can't make it back from the conference tonight. The company are paying for us to stay at a hotel so don't worry! Make sure you lock up and you should be fine. I'll try your mobile just in case, but I'll see you in the morning. Stay safe. Love you.'

She usually called the home phone thinking he would be most likely to see a message on his way in or out of the house. He found it amusing that they even had a landline as she was the only one who ever phoned it, but in fairness she was right. He felt his pockets and realised with no concern that his phone was still on his bed.

He didn't like that she hadn't made it back, but at least it wasn't like she was choosing to stay late in the lab, working on whatever her latest research project was. Thinking about it, he was a little glad she wasn't home. He hadn't wiped his internet searches from her laptop after online gaming earlier that evening, and he could only imagine how she'd react if she saw he was still trying to find his dad after eight years. *Someone has to*, he thought.

He wasn't mad that she didn't seem to search for him any more. He knew all too well that she missed him. Sometimes he'd hear her talking like his dad was in the room or find her staring at an old picture of them in the hallway. He tried not to let her catch him, but there was no way he was ready to give up looking. Surely anyone whose parent mysteriously vanished would be the same. He needed to know what had happened – to know he wasn't to blame.

He crossed through the kitchen, put on his shoes, and went into the garage where he shoved the metal sliding door up. Rain and wind hit him hard in the face. He shivered and braced himself, then dashed down the drive.

His footsteps were barely audible, and there was another boom of thunder as he picked up the wheelie bin and ran it inside. As he pulled the door back down, he laughed to himself at how soaked through he had become, and it was at this moment he felt the odd sensation of being watched.

Goosebumps sped across his arms. He glanced around the garage, nervous at the idea that someone could have snuck in when he had been outside. With no one else to be seen, he double checked the lock on the garage door before returning to the kitchen, promptly kicking off his shoes and locking the door behind him.

Only that afternoon he had reassured his mum he would be fine without her for the evening. He was twelve after all, but he hadn't counted on being alone all night or on feeling creeped out. Now he wasn't sure if he felt safe at all.

Rain continued to pelt down as another trail of lightning zigzagged across the dark night sky. A steady rumble of thunder rippled through the house like the aftermath of a giant's footstep.

Rather than imagine what might be lurking around any corner in a shadow, he stood for a moment in the kitchen and tried to calm his thoughts. As he began to feel at ease, he was distracted by the water dripping from his clothes to the floor and scowled at a sensation he truly hated – soggy socks.

He dressed for bed and listened to the other message from his mum on his mobile, then worked his way around the small bungalow, turning on the lights one by one to check for anything out of the ordinary. He was very careful to ensure all the windows and doors were locked. Then he cleared his browser history from his mum's laptop and went to bed.

As he switched on his lamp, several flashes of lightning lit up the room. Immediately afterwards, thunder exploded above with such force that his bedroom walls shook, and a large marble rolled off a shelf, thudding loudly as it hit the floor. He opened his mouth in awe, wishing he wasn't alone, and noticed the skirting board next to the marble. It was ... glowing?

His eyes traced the edges of the room to the gap at the bottom of his bedroom door. A peculiar blue-and-white light was shining through. *Could it be torchlight?* It lingered too long to be lightning. What if someone else was in the house after all?

He gulped and instinctively made himself still, breathing slowly so as not to make a sound. He listened hard but all he could hear was the storm.

The light under the door continued to shimmer brightly.

He picked up his phone but placed it back down. The last thing he wanted to do was call someone in the middle of the night and get in trouble for waking them up, especially if it turned out he was overreacting.

Instead, he crept quietly across the room and placed an ear to the door. There was no sound from the other side.

He looked around. There had to be something he could use to feel a bit safer. *Yes!* He lifted a tennis racket from the messy pile of things on the chair next to him. Then, with a little more confidence, he turned the door handle.

Peering through the gap, he saw the shimmering light on the walls and carpet but nothing else of concern, so holding the racket firmly he opened the door and stepped into the hallway.

Thunder rolled overhead, but he could hear something else. It sounded like ... a voice.

His heart thudded heavily in his chest.

He tiptoed down the hallway and stopped outside the glass-panelled door to the dining area. The light was shining through it from the living room.

'Fyn! Are you there?'

He froze and held his breath. There was a man in the house. Had he been there all this time? Fyn stepped back. How did he know his name?

'If you're there, I need to talk to you! It's okay. I won't hurt you!'

He wanted to stay still, but the man's tone sounded urgent. What if it was important? What if he was needed? Compelled, he stepped forward again, and then further still, until he found himself marvelling at an extraordinary sight.

Above the sofa he had been sleeping on not even half an hour earlier, and surrounded by crackling blue-and-white light, was what he could only have described as a circular hole in mid-air. It stood like a coin on its side and was nearly as wide as he was tall. In the centre of it, directly level with his face, was the head and upper body of a man. A man who was staring at him.

Their eyes connected as the man spoke again.

'Fyn? Is that you?' His rugged voice sounded relieved. He ran his fingers through his hair then down to his stubbly chin. 'Of course it is. I know this must be more than a shock, but I need you to listen.' He looked around as though trying to avoid being spotted.

Fyn could make out a rocky wall behind him in the dark, and he appeared to be outside, but in this bizarre image the weather was calm and there was no storm. Unable to grasp what was happening, he stepped back and bumped into a cabinet.

'You need to be careful!' the man continued.

Fyn glanced at the cabinet.

'I didn't mean that,' the man said. 'There are worse things out there than home furnishings. I *mean*, you need to pay attention to anyone new in your life. I think you'll be approached soon. Challenge anyone you're unsure of.'

The tennis racket slipped from Fyn's fingers to the carpet. He held his hands close to his chest and wiped the sweat from them on his top.

'I know it's scary,' the man continued, 'but it's vital that you listen. Can you do that for me?'

Fyn struggled to find words. 'Wh... who are you?' he stammered, his breathing now quick and shallow. 'I... I don't understand what's happening.' He closed his eyes and shook his head. When he opened them again the man looked sad.

'I'm so sorry to do it like this. I had no other way. There are horrible people out there, but I guess it takes all sorts to make a world.' He paused as though realising some truth. 'It's hard to describe. You need to watch out for the agents.'

'Who... who are the agents?' Fyn asked.

The man sighed. 'They could be anyone. They're most likely new to you. They'll try to make you trust them and...'

The sentence wasn't finished. An ear-splitting screech filled the air from inside the circle and the man turned to his right, looking at something beyond the view of Fyn. When he turned back, his eyes were wide with fear.

'I've got to go! Beware of the agents!' He ducked down and the circle closed in on itself, disappearing completely. No more blue-and-white light. No more mysterious man. All that remained was the now gentle rumbling of the passing storm and the sound of Fyn's shocked breathing.

He slid down the cabinet and sat gripping his legs, staring ahead at what once more appeared to be a perfectly normal living room.

CHAPTER TWO
The Calm After the Storm

Fyn's thoughts the next morning came slowly at first, but soon his mind was bombarded with details.

He had woken on the living-room floor sometime after sunrise and taken himself to bed. Now he found himself not wanting to believe what had happened, trying to convince himself that it had been nothing more than a bad dream.

With a yawn and a good stretch, he got up and dressed. Then he saw the tennis racket resting on the chair by the door. Had he really moved it? *What about...?* He looked on the floor and frowned as he saw the marble, exactly where it had settled the night before.

Fyn recalled the man's warning, *Beware of the agents*, but who were they? There was no one new in Fyn's life and he had no plans to meet anyone. It had to mean something. *Who was that man?*

A loud groan erupted from his stomach as he realised he could smell the smoky aroma of bacon. Trying to ignore the living room on the way, he wandered around to the kitchen where he found his mum bopping about as she cooked. Her mousy brown hair was tied back and, as usual, she had a pencil perched above her right ear.

'Hi, Mum. When did you get home?'

'Fyn!' She span around to see him and did a little boogie with the frying pan before taking out her headphones. Her skin was flushed pink from dancing. 'Welcome to your weekend! About an hour ago, I think. I'm sorry I didn't make it back last night. I absolutely hated the thought of you being home alone, but I knew you'd be okay. You are, aren't you? I thought I'd have to call in the troops to get you out of bed.'

'Troops?' He raised an eyebrow.

'Oh, I don't know,' she chuckled. 'You just seemed out for the count when I popped my head around the door earlier. Is everything alright? You look a little dazed.'

He didn't know where to begin and didn't want her to worry. 'I'm fine, thanks. Just tired. The storm kept me up late and I didn't sleep well.'

She placed a bacon sandwich in front of him with a bottle of tomato sauce.

'Thanks,' he said, smiling.

'You look like you could use a quiet day,' she said as she poured him some orange juice. 'Do you have much planned?'

'I'm seeing Amy this afternoon,' he replied. 'We're going to talk about staying at Grandad Bernie's when you're on your big trip. Oh!' He suddenly remembered her evening. 'How was your conference last night?'

Mrs Carter was a physicist and worked with Amy's parents at Future Planet Research Centre. It was quite rare for them to go away, but they had been planning a scientific expedition and were due to leave in a few days.

'Very good, thanks,' she replied as she wiped the worktop. 'Apart from old Professor Harrow. He always feels the need to stick his oar in and last night was no exception. I don't know why he can't just stuff a sponge in that cake hole and give us some peace!'

Fyn laughed. 'What did he do this time?'

'Same old, same old. He's so stingy and all over the budget like we haven't been planning the trip for years! I'd love to...' She seemed to think better of finishing her sentence. 'Let's just say he isn't making any friends, and a few friends might do him good. Thanks for bringing in the bin by the way.'

The change in topic brought him back to Earth with a bang. So that had happened too.

'Fyn?'

'Ah, sorry, Mum.' He realised he was making a vague expression. 'I've just got some stuff on my mind. No problem about the bin.'

'Are you worried about the expedition?'

Fyn felt himself tense up. 'No, I'm fine. Really.'

She sat next to him.

He gulped. *Here it comes*.

'I know your dad disappeared on a work trip,' she said softly, 'and I know I have the same sort of job as he did, but it *will* be fine. We've thought everything through. Actually, we've double, triple, and quadruple checked. We won't take any risks, and I wouldn't go if I thought there was any danger.'

'I know,' he said, wishing she hadn't brought up his dad. He wanted to support her, but the thought of her going away did bother him a bit. If only his parents had chosen boring careers. Maybe then his life would be different. His dad wouldn't be gone. His mum wouldn't distract herself with work. In Fyn's opinion, science had a lot to answer for.

The truth was that he couldn't bear the idea of her not coming home, even though she'd been on trips like this before and he was mostly sure she'd be okay. Her work was important to her. That's why he would never tell her how he really felt about it.

'You still can't say where you'll be?' he asked.

'You know I can't,' she replied. 'It's not a matter of trust. It's just a very strict company policy. We can talk all about it as much as you like when I'm back. I promise.'

He smiled half-heartedly.

'Anything else you want to talk about?' she asked.

'No, thanks,' he said. 'I'm okay.'

She gave him an uncertain look but didn't say anything else on it. 'Alright. Well, I'm going to cross-reference some notes in the garden. Don't overdo it today.' She picked up her cup of tea and went outside.

Later that afternoon, Fyn was already sweating from the heat and had only walked the few streets from his house to Amy's. Other than some damaged fencing and roughed up bushes, there were practically no signs that a storm had been in the area less than twelve hours earlier.

He pressed the doorbell and a silhouette in the frosted glass told him Amy's dad, Mark Patterson, was about to answer. Sure enough, he was greeted by a tall, pale man with green eyes, short black hair, and a cheesy grin.

'Fyn! Come on in!' Mr Patterson stepped aside and let him through. 'Excuse the ... well the ... err...'. Mr Patterson gestured around him. The hallway and stairs were covered in small piles of clothing, notepads, sleeping bags, electronics, and bizarre pieces of equipment. Crates and suitcases were dotted around between everything else and were in the process of being filled. 'We've started packing for the big trip and Chloe likes to...'

'Likes to *what?*' Amy's mum, Chloe Patterson, called down the stairs in a slightly harassed voice, her Jamaican accent sounding thicker than usual.

'Oh, ummm ... nothing dear! I was just telling Fyn how thorough you're being.'

'I'm sure that's *exactly* what you were telling him,' she replied. 'We need to pack it all. It's in the name of science!'

Mr Patterson gave Fyn a knowing look and whispered, 'Maybe, but I'm not sure about the number of shoes.'

Fyn smiled.

'Hi, Fyn,' Mrs Patterson called down to him. 'Come in out of the heat. Amy's in the attic and there's ice cream in the freezer.'

'Thanks, Mrs P!' he called back up. Then he gave Mr Patterson a polite shrug before carefully navigating his way around the random piles to the stairs.

When he reached the landing, he saw Mrs Patterson in her room, sorting through a suitcase.

'Good to see you!' she said, looking over to him. 'Excuse any tension. We're just a little behind after getting caught up last night. Were you okay at home? Did your mum make it back alright this morning?'

'Fine, thanks,' he replied.

'I'm glad. Now, excuse me ... I need to find my...' She trailed off as she disappeared out of sight.

'Hey!'

Fyn looked around and spotted Amy's head poking out of the attic, her curly black hair spiralling from the ceiling, and her brown eyes wide with impatience.

'Fyn! We *so* need to talk! Get up here!' Her face and hair withdrew back into the attic, and he climbed up to join her.

'I'm glad you're here,' she said. 'Did you see the storm last night?' It was *amazing!* It's been so long since we've had one like that. I nearly wet my pants!'

He laughed, and her bronze freckle-covered face lit up.

'Yes, it was pretty crazy,' he replied, slightly subdued. 'It shook the walls at home and everything.'

She stared in disbelief. 'Noooo! That's awesome! Why aren't you more excited about it?'

He shuffled his feet a bit. Now that it came to it, he wasn't sure talking about the events of the night before was a good idea.

She narrowed her eyes. 'Storms don't usually bother you. What's up? Was it the being home alone thing?'

'No, it's nothing. I'm just tired. What are you doing up here anyway?' He was changing the subject, and he knew it. She liked to spend her time in the attic because she considered it more interesting than anything as boring as 'normal'.

'Urgh!' she groaned. 'I just wanted to escape the parentals and their packing. She rolled her eyes and let herself fall backwards to rest on an old beanbag. Her long gangly legs hung over the edge as the beans shuffled inside. 'How ready are you for staying at your grandad's?'

'I've not really done anything yet,' he admitted. 'You?'

'Same. It's so hot I can't bear the thought of packing.'

He nodded but wasn't really listening. It was now or never. 'Err... There is something I kind of wanted to talk to you about.' He paused before deciding to continue. 'It might sound a bit crazy though.'

She sat up, scrunching the bean bag into another position.

'Go on,' she prompted.

'Well...'

He told her everything he remembered from the night before. The only tweak he made was saying that, although it felt real, he was sure it must have been a dream.

She gave him a bit of a look afterwards, like the one his mum had given him that morning.

'I don't think there's anything to worry about,' she said. 'Maybe you just ate too late and had trapped wind or something. Last time I had trapped wind I dreamt Dad was a flamenco dancer and *that* was scary! I think it sounds like you just need a good night's sleep.'

'You don't think it could mean something more? The dream, I mean.'

'Like what?' she asked.

He found himself shifting again. It had just occurred to him that maybe, just maybe, this *was* some kind of message, and if it really was a message then what if it was connected to his dad? After so many years, could the man who had appeared be some clue to his dad's whereabouts? What if the very agents he had been warned about were actually a key to finding out more? He felt a rush of excitement pulse through him as new ideas began to click into place.

'Like what?' Amy asked again.

'Well, I don't know but what if—'

'—Oh, Fyn. Not your dad again?'

He sighed. She was always telling him to stop looking for his dad, telling him it wasn't good for him and that if he wanted to be found he would turn up.

'You never know!' he said. 'This could mean something!'

'Or it could be you getting your hopes up again!' she replied, shaking her head with disapproval.

'There's nothing wrong with hope,' he protested.

'I know that,' she said, 'and I hate to say it, but maybe you should hope for things that are more likely to actually happen.'

Too afraid to admit Amy might be right, he didn't say anything more on it. Instead, he moved the conversation on, and they spent the rest of the afternoon chatting, eating ice cream, and playing retro games on some of Mr Patterson's old consoles.

CHAPTER THREE

Written in the Stars

A few days later as Fyn's mum drove them to Grandad Bernie's house, Fyn and Amy spent their time chatting, requesting songs from their playlists, and watching the scenery gradually change. They had left the larger towns behind them and were surrounded by country hills and enormous fields, rich in crops of green and yellow.

After a while, Amy took her diary from her bag and began to make notes. Fyn focused on a small mark on the window, lifting and lowering his head to give the impression it was flying above the horizon alongside them as he let his mind wander.

Amy still refused to listen to the idea that he had dreamt up a message which might relate to his dad, but his visit from the stranger was all he'd been able to think about. Every time he saw someone he didn't recognise, he wondered if they could be an agent, and at night he was on constant alert for the return of the mysterious messenger.

'Nearly there,' his mum said as they reached a small village.

'Thank goodness,' he replied, looking at her reflection in the rear-view mirror.

'Second that,' said Amy, sitting up straighter. 'I've got a numb bum.'

They passed through the village and back to narrow roads, and after about ten more minutes they pulled on to a long gravel track surrounded by tall oak trees.

'Here we are,' his mum said, following the curve of the track to the left.

The trees cleared and Fyn felt a glow of excitement as he saw Grandad Bernie's house.

The warm red-and-brown brick walls were wrapped in dark green ivy which flowed all the way up to the terracotta tiled roof. The front garden was full of colourful flower beds and well-trimmed bushes. A waist-high stone wall ran around it to an emerald-green gate which opened on to the front path.

His mum turned to face them from the driver's seat. 'Before we head in, I just wanted to check you two are alright. No last minute concerns? I know it's a bit late in the day, but just in case.'

'All good,' Fyn replied. 'You know Grandad. We'll be fine.'

'That I do.' She smiled. 'How about you, Amy?'

'Fine here, Mrs C,' she answered. 'I'm just ready for sunshine and country adventure! But don't worry...' she added quickly, '... nothing *too* out there.'

'That's what I like to hear,' she replied. 'Now look, just enjoy yourselves and make the most of the break. You'll be fine and...' her voice wavered a little, '...we'll be back before you know it.'

'Are *you* okay?' Fyn asked her.

'Of course!' she replied before clearing her throat. 'Right then you two! Let's get your stuff.'

They collected their belongings and were walking up the garden path when the front door of the house swung wide open. Grandad Bernie was standing in the doorway, beaming at them all. He had a full head of short white hair, covered with a grey tweed flat cap. His hair was matched with a trimmed white beard and moustache that stood out against his age-worn skin. He was heavily tanned from many hours in the garden and, much to Fyn's delight, was wearing the '*Call me Vintage*' jumper Fyn and his mum had bought him for his birthday a few years ago.

One by one, he embraced them all. 'You're looking more like your father every time I see you,' he said proudly as he reached Fyn. 'Same messy brown hair. Same blue eyes. Just like me when I was your age! You could do with a bit more sun though,' he teased. 'Have you been hiding away with your computer games?'

Fyn gave him a cheeky grin.

'Carol, are you stopping in?' Grandad Bernie asked. 'It would be great if you could stay for tea.'

'I'd love to,' she replied.

They moved the bags into the hallway, placing them at the bottom of the stairs.

Family photographs taken over many years adorned the walls, and ornaments from Grandad Bernie's earlier travels sat on an assortment of mismatched units by a tall grandfather clock. There was an older feel about the place, but it was charming, and Fyn loved it. It was like the house itself welcomed him in, encouraging him to relax.

They went into the kitchen and sat at the table as Grandad Bernie began preparing drinks.

'I've been looking forward to seeing you all ever since we planned it,' he said. 'It's been so long since we last saw each other.'

He knew it wasn't said with any resentment, but Fyn couldn't help feeling a little guilty. He would have loved to see his grandad more, but school and distance didn't make it easy. He wrote to him from time to time and joined in on his mum's phone calls, but he couldn't help wondering if he felt lonely living on his own.

'I've really missed you too, Grandad,' he said with extra emphasis, trying to show he meant it.

Grandad Bernie smiled and scuffed up Fyn's hair with a tea towel. 'I know that, short stuff. You don't need to remind me.'

'How's your summer been, Bernie?' Fyn's mum asked.

'Lovely, thanks,' he replied, 'but not especially eventful – apart from a series of mysterious thefts at the local grocery shop!'

'Thefts?' Amy asked.

'Well, not quite,' Grandad Bernie admitted. 'It turned out someone's Labrador was sneaking in and snacking on food from the lower shelves.'

They chuckled as he brought them their drinks.

Fyn's mum stayed for an evening barbecue in the garden. When she finished her coffee and started clearing her plate aside Fyn felt suddenly empty, and it wasn't long before they were standing on the path at the front of the house.

'I'll look forward to catching up when you're back,' said Grandad Bernie holding her close, 'and don't worry about the kids. We'll have a grand time.'

She laughed. 'That's what I'm worried about.'

'I hope it all goes well, Mrs C,' said Amy. 'Please send my love to my mum and dad, but you know ... not in a cheesy way.'

'I'll do my best,' she replied, hugging Amy goodbye.

Fyn went with his mum to the car while the others waited at the house. He looked up at her and they shared an awkward sort of smile, knowing this part never seemed to get easier.

'It's going to be alright,' she said. 'You know we won't be able to phone or email when we arrive at our base. We can't afford to interfere with signals or the data we're collecting. I doubt we'll have access to a post box either, but I promise we'll try.'

'I know...' he said quietly. 'I hope everything goes okay.'

'I'm sure it will,' she replied, perking up a little. 'I've got a good feeling about this one. In the meantime, make the most of your summer holidays. We'll need to get you ready for school when I'm home.'

He frowned and pushed going back to school out of his mind as he gave her the biggest hug he thought he could get away with.

She held him tight, kissed him on the cheek, and then turned to intensely adjust the wing mirror on the car.

He heard her sniff a little before she looked back.

'You'll be okay, kiddo.'

'I know, Mum. Back at you.'

'Thanks,' she said, smiling with slightly watery eyes. 'Love you.'

'Love you too.'

Then she got in the car, wound down the window, and blew them all dramatic kisses as she drove along the gravel pathway and beyond the tree line.

An hour or so later, Fyn was lying on the bed in his dad's old bedroom and letting his eyes follow the stippled pattern on the ceiling.

He and Amy had decided to escape to their rooms and sort their things while Grandad Bernie watched the news downstairs.

The room was light and airy with large windows that opened to the garden and surrounding countryside. Old shelves were full of his dad's childhood books, and over the years Fyn had read them all. Somehow, it made him feel closer to him again.

He looked at a photo on the bedside table and felt a slight pang of emotion. It was of Fyn when he was four years old, on a day out with his parents. He didn't remember it being taken, but he knew it was from a few months before his dad disappeared. *Before he abandoned us*, he tried not to think, although it was better than most other people thought. Most people thought he had died.

A welcome breeze flowed gently through the window.

He closed his eyes, let his mind settle, and was soon on the verge of dozing off when there was a knock on the bedroom door. He looked over and saw Amy's long hair swaying to the side as she tilted her head into the room.

'I'm sorry. I didn't mean to wake you.'

'It's okay. I... wasn't sleeping... just... yet,' he replied, stifling a yawn. 'Is everything okay?'

'All good. Grandad Bernie's making hot chocolate. We wondered if you wanted some?'

He leapt off the bed, remembering the way Grandad Bernie always made it from scratch.

They found him at the stove, warming milk in a pan. It was dark outside, but the kitchen was softly lit by an old yellow light bulb.

'All settled in?' he asked, looking up at them.

Fyn nodded.

'That's great. I thought you'd like some hot chocolate – if you're not too old for it. There are biscuits too.' He pointed to a tin on the table and winked. 'They're the good ones.'

'Love it,' said Amy.

'Thanks,' said Fyn, heading straight for them.

'I'm glad to know some things don't change,' Grandad Bernie said as he added a bit more chocolate to the milk.

'Anyway, I thought we could sit out for a bit. It's cooler but not bad. We can keep the back light on.'

As they settled around the garden table and under the twinkling stars, he raised his mug to toast them. 'It really is great to have you both stay again. It brings life to the old place.'

They raised their mugs in return.

'Are you happy out here, Grandad?' Fyn asked, unable to help himself.

Amy paused mid-sip.

'Oh yes,' he replied, looking up at the sky. 'You needn't worry about me. Honestly, I mean that, but there's always room for family.' He looked back at Fyn. 'It's just, apart from the thieving Labrador, the most action around here is, well... that's about it really.' He sighed heavily, took a sip of his drink, and started on a biscuit. 'I'm so beyond grateful for the experiences I've had in life, but sometimes... and don't get me wrong because I'm absolutely fine... but sometimes, I wonder if my best days are behind me.'

'Grandad!' said Fyn, slightly alarmed. 'No way. There's so much more to come. We'll show you, won't we Amy?'

She had been dunking a biscuit for so long it broke off and bobbed in her drink.

'Absolutely,' she agreed, 'and a thieving Labrador is far more exciting than anything we've had back home – apart from the recent storm anyway.'

Fyn felt a shiver run through him.

'Not too cold?' Grandad Bernie asked.

'No, no,' he replied, trying to brush past it. 'Just a shiver.'

Amy leaned across the table, and in her best spooky voice warbled, 'Maybe someone walked over your grave...'

He shrugged and flicked a large crumb at her.

'It doesn't matter if they did,' Grandad Bernie said matter-of-factly. 'I always say our loved ones never truly leave us. Maybe it's a distant relative.'

'You're suggesting someone *actually* walked over my grave?' Fyn asked, giving Grandad Bernie an uncertain look.

'Excellent,' Amy whispered, as her floating biscuit sank unnoticed beneath the surface of her drink.

'Well, it's like your Grandmother Francine used to say, "there's so much energy inside us. Even when we're asleep our bodies chug away, so when we die, where does all that energy go?". I like to think she's still with me somehow, even if it's just her energy brightening up the place.'

Fyn thought about it. His Grandma Frannie had died before he was born, but even though he was sad they hadn't met, he'd heard so much about her that he felt close to her somehow. It was true that there was a positive feeling in the house. Maybe there was more to it. The thought gave him hope. He definitely didn't feel like his dad was around, so maybe the worst hadn't happened. Maybe they *would* find him someday.

'What do you think happens to us?' Amy asked, carrying on the conversation.

'I couldn't tell you,' said Grandad Bernie, 'but we'll all find out some day.'

The three of them sat in silence for a moment, looking up at the stars before he spoke again. 'Francine used to love the sky. She'd say it was always different, day to day and season to season because, even though it can look the same, the air is always moving.'

He looked at them as if to check their understanding, but Fyn and Amy stared back blankly.

'I think what she felt,' he continued, 'is there's more to life than what we see, or at least that we're part of a bigger picture. Maybe there is something connecting the dots.'

'Like destiny?' asked Amy.

'Hmmm,' said Grandad Bernie. 'Are our lives written in the stars?' He paused again, and Fyn suspected he was trying to build some playful tension. 'Perhaps we shouldn't get *too* deep on day one. I think it's time for us to head back in, don't you?'

As they made their way inside for the night, Fyn glanced up again at the thousands of stars above and wondered what the bigger picture might be.

Chapter Four

A Discovery in the Woods

'Morning! Did you hear from your mum?' Amy asked Fyn as she joined him at the top of the stairs. 'My mum and dad said they got to the airport okay.'

He nodded. 'She said they'll be in touch when their plane lands, but I don't know when that will be…'

She huffed. 'Isn't it so annoying? I guess that's the trouble with "secret and strictly classified" expeditions.'

'Exactly,' he replied, trying again not to think of the way his dad disappeared on one. It was so weird not knowing where his mum would be.

They found Grandad Bernie doing a crossword at the kitchen table.

'Good morning you two,' he said, looking up at them. 'Can I get you anything for breakfast?'

'Morning,' said Fyn, walking over to the pantry. 'I'll get it, thanks. Do you want anything?'

'Not for me, ta,' he replied before filling in an answer and putting his pen down. 'I ate a while ago. Us oldies need to make the most of our days, so I've been up for hours. Everything's in the usual place.'

Fyn and Amy prepared marmalade on toast with a side of plump, fresh strawberries, before working out their plans for the day. Grandad Bernie wanted to pop to the village and buy bulbs for some gardening, so they decided to head out in the afternoon while he did that.

Carrying their backpacks, they left through the back gate and headed down to the fields below. There were no roads ahead for miles. When they reached the bottom of the slope, Fyn launched straight into a field of dry grass.

'Race you to the other side!' he shouted, running with no cares in the world, only the warm breeze on his face, the hot sun on his skin, and the tickly scratches of grass on his legs. It was glorious, and much more fun than his recent busy thoughts.

Amy soon caught up to him. 'That's so unfair!' she called. 'You got a major head start!', but they both laughed until the ache from a stitch in his side forced Fyn to slow down.

She overtook with glee, stopping only to let him catch up. 'Still a loser though,' she added with a cheeky grin.

'Pffft!' he exhaled, catching his breath. 'Who was racing?'

They came to a shallow stream with large rocks scattered across it. As they had so many times as younger children, they crossed by balancing their way to the other side.

Then Fyn paused. He'd never been beyond this point.

Feeling further from Grandad Bernie's than expected, he steadied himself, felt the thrill of freedom in his heart, and launched onwards again towards some woods in the distance.

Reaching the shade of the trees, he grinned. Rays of sunlight shining through the foliage lit patches of the ground ahead. It didn't look too bad. 'Are you sure you want to go in?'

Amy shrugged, and together they stepped past the tree line, their footsteps breaking noisily upon twigs and old fallen leaves as birds sang merrily in the treetops above.

After a while they came to a gentle incline, and the further up it they went, the lighter the woods became. When the trees cleared, they found themselves back in the sunshine, on top of a large hill overlooking more country fields.

Far away, tiny-looking cottages with thatched roofs were dotted here and there, and winding hedgerows hid a curving country lane where he could just about make out the top of a tractor chugging along slowly. Further still, a solitary red windmill stood proudly like the centrepiece of a grand display.

'Shall we stop here?' he asked, thinking it felt like a good spot.

'Sure,' Amy replied, settling down and making herself comfortable on the grass. She took off her trainers and socks, stretching out her feet.

Fyn sat and stared at the horizon. It felt so freeing to be out in the middle of nowhere, but recent events still pulled at his mind. He had no clues and nothing to work with. It was like he was caught on one side of a wall, knowing that everything he wanted was behind it.

He had tried searching for 'agents' online but that was no help at all, and whenever he searched for things like 'people appearing in portals and wormholes', the results ranged massively. He'd gone from feeling like he had a chance to wondering if it would ever present itself again.

'You're still thinking about it, aren't you?' Amy asked.

'I can't help it,' he admitted.

'I know,' she said, somewhat surprising him.

'I *am* on your side.' She laughed, imitating his raised eyebrows. 'I just don't like seeing it bug you like this. Your dad left years ago. You can't let it stop you from living your life.'

Fyn looked down at the grass, hoping to avoid her serious face, but when he looked back at her it was relaxed – sincere.

Amy had been his best friend since preschool when she built an epic sandcastle and let him use it for his action figures. He didn't have any other proper friends now, but he didn't feel like he needed anyone else.

'Thanks,' he said, before looking back at the horizon.

She ripped up a handful of grass and threw it at him.

He turned back to her, but she threw another handful. This time some went in his mouth. He spluttered and spat it out as she burst into laughter. Unable to help himself, he started laughing too.

Seeming to be satisfied that he had listened to her, Amy pulled a book out of her bag and began to read.

Lying on the grass, Fyn closed his eyes and faced the sky. The warm sunlight shone red through his eyelids. Perhaps there was something to this "living your life" business after all.

Once the novelty of getting outside had worn off, they packed up and began the journey back.

They were walking calmly near the edge of the woods closest to Grandad Bernie's, when a dog began to bark aggressively nearby.

Panicked birds burst into the sky. Then ... silence.

'Not loving that,' said Amy, her voice barely louder than a whisper. 'Let's not hang about.'

Fyn felt the same. He was suddenly aware of how alone they were, hidden from the outside world among the trees. As they walked on, every step felt louder than their last, and every crunch beneath their feet came with the potential to bring unwanted attention.

A yelp stopped them in their tracks.

Something thrashed about behind some bushes. Then there was silence again.

'What do you think it was?' Amy whispered.

He whispered back. 'I'm not sure... Do you think we should check?'

She looked as convinced as he felt, which wasn't very much, but he knew they wouldn't leave an animal in need.

'Okay,' she replied, 'but let's be careful.'

'Here,' said Fyn, picking up a couple of sturdy-looking sticks and passing one to Amy. Trying not to let his nerves get the better of him, he smiled at her encouragingly. Then, slowly, they crept around the side of the bushes.

Amy gasped and dashed forward, stopping in the middle of a clearing.

'Fyn! Look at it! It's really hurt!'

Reaching her side he spotted, just a few metres away, a wounded young fox lying against the base of a tree. Blood was seeping from its neck and its eyes were closed. Hearing them approach, it opened them weakly, lifting its head slightly to look at them. If it wanted to growl a warning to keep them away, it didn't. Perhaps it couldn't. It slumped its head back down and lay still.

'What should we do?' she asked.

'I don't know,' he said softly. 'I don't want to scare it.'

'What about Grandad Bernie?' she suggested.

'Maybe,' he replied. 'He should be home by now.' He pulled his phone out of his pocket and saw it had no signal.

Amy's was the same. She looked back at the fox and to Fyn. 'Will you be okay if I run for it? If Grandad Bernie's there I'll bring him back. If not, I don't know... I'll sort something! Will you stay here?'

'No problem,' he replied, not sure he wanted to be left alone. 'Just make sure you find your way back.'

'I won't be long,' she said, leaving the clearing.

He heard her break into a run then looked back to the fox.

It didn't move.

Quietly, he unzipped his backpack and tried searching for something which could help, but there was nothing of use.

He wanted to rush to it – give it support – but felt that might panic it. Instead, to try and be less intimidating, he gently lowered himself to sit on the dry earth.

'Hello, you,' he said calmly, still a few metres away. 'What happened?' Then, realising whatever caused its injuries could still be nearby, he peered over his shoulder.

Thankful for no further sign of danger, he looked back to the fox which remained still.

A sense of unease built within him. He didn't know the best thing to do. He tried to relax, hoping it would project some level of comfort, but he saw the blood and the way the fox's breathing was slowing.

'I'm sure Amy won't be long,' he said, more to himself than the fox. He fidgeted with his fingers, moving his thumbs between them, feeling helpless as he waited.

A crunch of leaves came from the ground behind him.

Carefully, he raised himself to a crouching position and turned.

In the gap between a tree and bush he and Amy had just walked by, and where he had looked only moments ago, there was a large black-and-brown dog.

Thick drool mixed with blood dribbled from its teeth, and it stared at him as though daring him to move.

Fyn understood how the fox had been injured.

Thoughts raced through his mind. What if the dog had a taste for blood? What if it hadn't finished what it started?

The dog growled as though it could tell what he was thinking.

Fyn's hands felt clammy. He was sure that his heart was beating faster. What if the dog could hear that too?

Then there was another sound of breaking leaves from behind the bush and a tall, slim man stepped into view.

Chapter Five

Wild Things

'Hey!' the man called gruffly to the dog.

It ran to his feet.

'I see you've met Samson,' he added, looking at Fyn crouching on the ground. 'Don't worry,' he said with a wry smile. 'He wouldn't hurt a fly.'

Fyn wanted to look back at the fox but thought better of taking his eyes away from the stranger and his dog.

Instead, the stranger did it for him, looking at the fox with a gleam in his eyes. He stroked Samson roughly on the head, and Samson's bloody slobber dribbled to the floor in a thick gloop. 'Well ... he has to have a little sport every now and then.'

Fyn was disgusted but held his tongue. He gripped the stick in his hand firmly as he stood up.

Samson glared at him, transfixed, and the man exhaled a short breath, like a semi-impressed laugh. 'Got a bit of an edge to you? I respect that.'

Fyn guessed he was in his late forties. He was wearing beige walking trousers and a grubby green jumper. His thinning hair was spread to the side in a bad attempt at a comb-over, but Fyn doubted anyone would point it out. He didn't look like the kind of person anyone would want to upset.

'Anyway,' the man continued, casually leaning his shoulder against the tree, 'what could a lad like you be doing out in the woods on your own like this? I can't help but think it seems quite...' he smiled as he chose his next word '...suspicious. Come on. Speak up!'

Fyn couldn't believe it. To be told that his behaviour seemed suspicious by someone as wildly suspicious as him was outrageous.

'I'm exploring,' he said, doing his best to keep his nerve but feeling wary. 'That's all. What about you and your dog?' A thought flashed through his mind – was this just some random slightly disturbing stranger, or could he be one of the agents? He didn't look much like an agent to Fyn. At least not in the way he imagined. He'd pictured someone smarter – possibly in a suit.

The man smiled widely. It wasn't pleasant. 'Actually, Fyn, I was looking for you. I was hoping we could ... chat.'

Fyn felt winded, suddenly more vulnerable. How did he know him? He *had* to be an agent, but then … the man in his living room had known his name too, and *he* had warned against agents.

'Don't worry,' the man said casually. 'I'm here to help.' He rubbed Samson's head vigorously as the dog continued to glare at Fyn.

'I… I don't need help, thanks,' Fyn stammered, but the man didn't seem to care.

'Of course you wouldn't *think* you need help, but that's because you don't know what you need help with.'

'Who *are* you?' Fyn asked, wondering how long it would take Amy to get back, and if she would bring Grandad Bernie.

'Forgive me,' the man said. 'My name is Martin, and I am … a friend of sorts.' He flashed his yellow teeth into another nasty grin.

'What do you want?' Fyn asked.

'All in time, but…' he seemed to reconsider, '…perhaps you could be right. I'll listen to my instincts. It might sound strange, and I don't want you to … what do young people say? Freak out? I work for a powerful organisation who have tasked me with informing you that someone may try to contact you. That someone will seem like they're on your side, but you must ignore them.' He studied Fyn's face for any hint of recognition.

Fyn thought again of the man from the circle of light in his living room.

Martin continued with a satisfied smile. 'So, it has happened.'

'No, I...'

'I keep telling you Fyn, don't worry. You can tell me *anything*. We're friends.' He knelt and started scratching Samson's belly with his dirty fingernails.

Samson submitted happily.

'The thing is, Fyn, whoever contacts you will try to make you feel like they should be trusted. They may even try to trick you with something familiar. Something you care about.' He sounded like the idea was ridiculous. 'Do not believe them. They are keeping you from the truth. They'll draw you in by focusing on your interests. Whatever touches your heart. Whatever you love.'

Fyn didn't want to listen but found himself intrigued. Should he trust the man from his living room or the creepy man in front of him now? He needed to know more.

'If you're right, and someone does try to contact me...'

'I am right, Fyn, and someone already has contacted you. Let's not play games.'

'What do you want me to do?'

'It's quite simple. Do not trust them. Do not do what they ask. Stay away from them, and treat them like a bug on the bottom of your shoe. That will be as good as they deserve.'

'Why should I trust you?' Fyn asked. 'How do you even know who I am? Why are you telling me all of this?'

'Give it time. Then you'll sense the truth of my words.'

Fyn huffed. 'Why can't someone just tell me what's going on?' Then he wondered if he'd pushed too far as Martin's face turned stony.

'Fyn!'

It was Amy.

Samson leapt up and growled in her direction.

Fyn turned to spot her, but she wasn't in sight yet. He could just about hear her running towards him.

'I'll be in touch,' said Martin. He flashed another toothy grin. 'Remember what I've said. I'll know if you don't.'

Then, followed by Samson who looked back with a snarl, he left the clearing.

Amy shouted again. 'Fyn!'

'I'm over here,' he called back, trying not to disturb the fox too much.

She arrived in the clearing with Grandad Bernie just behind her. He was out of breath and carrying an old cat carrier with a blanket in it.

'How is...' she broke off. 'Has something happened? Are you okay?' She looked around to see the fox and stopped talking.

Its eyes remained closed, and its body was still.

Grandad Bernie stepped calmly towards it, and carefully placed the cat carrier on the ground. Then he put on some gloves and held his hand gently against the fox before looking back at them. 'It was awake when you found it?'

'Yes,' they replied.

'That's not a good sign. It would have run if capable. Foxes don't usually keep close company with people.'

'How is it now?' Amy asked.

'It's hard to tell,' he replied, but his face was downcast and his tone serious. 'It's only a few months old and probably hasn't been on its own for long. We'll take it home and call the rescue centre. They might not get to it in time if we leave it here. Hopefully they can get it fixed up.'

'Wait,' said Fyn. 'There's something else.'

As Grandad Bernie wrapped the fox delicately in the blanket and placed it in the cat carrier, Fyn told them about his encounter with Martin and Samson. He didn't mention Martin's warning or that Martin knew his name. He would tell Amy later and see what she said.

'There's no way that we'll find him now,' said Grandad Bernie. 'Not that we should be searching for someone like that. We'll call the police, and...' he frowned, '...it's probably best you don't come out this far for the rest of your stay. Keep within view of the house.'

Fyn didn't need telling twice.

None of them said much as they returned to Grandad Bernie's, but Fyn replayed Martin's words in his mind, *I'll be in touch.*

Hopefully not too soon, he thought.

Chapter Six

Henry Flame

When they arrived home, the first thing Grandad Bernie did was call the rescue centre. Minutes later he set off in his old Jeep to take the fox to them.

'Stay in until I'm back,' he said as he left.

Amy sat drumming her fingers on the kitchen table. 'I'm sure it will be okay. I mean ... if we got to it in time.'

Fyn poured them some orange squash. 'I think we were there right away. We just need to hope that its wounds weren't too serious.'

'They did look serious though,' she said frowning. She slapped her hands on the table, nearly spilling their drinks. 'I can't believe anyone would let their dog do that! Who knows what else it might have done? It could have really hurt you!'

'Listen, Amy,' he started. 'There's more to it than I've let on. The man, I mean Martin... He knew my name.'

'*What?*' she shrieked. 'Why didn't you say something? He could know where you live! He could know where we are right now!' She got up and hurried to look out the back window.

'I know and I'll explain. Just please come and sit back down. I don't think he's coming anywhere near us, not yet anyway.'

She looked like she wanted to rant, but she returned to the table, sat firmly on her hands, and stared at him.

'He said I'd be contacted by someone else, and that I should stay away from them because I couldn't trust them.'

'I wouldn't trust anything *he* says,' said Amy, shaking her head.

'I didn't tell him it had already happened, but he worked it out.'

He waited for her to say something, knowing her mind would be on overload.

'Anyway,' he continued when she said nothing, 'the last thing I want to do is stress Grandad Bernie out. He doesn't know what I told you – about what happened that night in my living room.'

Amy made a face as though she had been asked to work out sixty-seven multiplied by one hundred and thirty-five in her head.

'What?' he asked.

'I'm torn,' she admitted. 'It sounds like there probably *was* someone in your house that night, but I just can't believe it! I mean, it sounds crazy.' She looked suddenly guilty. 'Not that you're crazy. It's just I was worried. You thought it might have been a dream, so I went with that. I never imagined it might have really happened.' She took a sip of her drink and put the glass down so absentmindedly some squash spilled over the table.

Fyn grabbed a tea towel and passed it to her. 'It's okay,' he said, relieved she was finally starting to listen.

'What does it all mean?' she asked as she wiped the table. 'What did he say again? The man you think you saw in your living room?'

'All he really managed to tell me is to be careful of any new people in my life. He said they could be agents. Then something interrupted him.'

'Agents?' she replied, staring into an empty space. 'Maybe Martin is an agent.'

'That's what I thought,' said Fyn. 'Plus, he said he worked for a powerful organisation.'

She looked back to him. 'The truth is we don't know if we can trust anyone we meet. Possible-Living-Room-Man said it. Scary-Woods-Man said it. I wonder who they are.'

Fyn ignored the "possible" comment. 'I wish I knew. I'm sure it's related to my dad somehow.'

'Maybe,' said Amy, 'but there's no proof of that just yet.'

'You mean you *still* don't believe me? After everything that's happened?'

She scowled. 'It's not that I don't believe you. It's just I want a bit more to go on before we link it to your dad. Don't forget I'm on your side.'

'Hmmm,' he mumbled. It didn't feel like it.

'Hey!' she said, her shoulders dropping. 'Don't be stupid. We're besties. I'm not letting you deal with this alone. Okay?'

He didn't reply.

She nudged him on the arm. '*Okay?*'

'Okay,' he said giving in, 'and sorry. I am grateful. I just want answers.'

'You and me both,' she said, 'and I'm sure we'll get them. Plus...' her eyes lit up with renewed energy – a mad sense of excitement coming from within, '...you have to admit, this is the closest thing to an adventure we've ever had!'

He couldn't help but smile. 'True. Although I'd always thought an adventure would be more fun.'

'It hasn't really started yet,' she replied as she returned to drumming her fingers on the table.

'He has a mild concussion and lost some blood,' said Grandad Bernie when he arrived home from the rescue centre a little later, 'but the wound looked worse than it is.'

'Will he be okay?' Amy asked.

'He's been through a lot for such a young fox, but hopefully he'll be fine. They've cleaned him up nicely.'

A sense of relief rushed over Fyn. 'What happens now?'

'They're going to watch him overnight but are a bit overwhelmed to be honest. Apparently, there have been a few similar incidents recently.'

'I wonder what caused those,' Amy remarked, rolling her eyes.

'At least they know more now,' said Grandad Bernie. 'I also called the police while I was there and told them what happened. They're going to up their patrols and distribute posters to warn the locals.'

'That's good,' said Fyn. He couldn't bear the thought of Samson attacking anything else.

'I have some other good news,' said Grandad Bernie. 'At least I think you'll like it. If the little chap is looking well enough in the morning, we'll be having him stay with us, just to keep an eye on him and make sure his wound doesn't get infected.'

'Are you serious?' asked Amy. 'That's awesome!'

'Very serious,' he replied. 'The rescue centre could do with the help. How does that sound to you, Fyn?'

'Great!' he said, but that night he found it hard to get to sleep. He was in two minds about whether to tell Grandad Bernie that Martin knew his name. On one hand, it would be good to warn him that there could be more to the situation, but on the other it would raise questions he wasn't ready for. His mum had phoned from the airport earlier and was excited for her expedition. The last thing he wanted to do was interrupt her plans. He decided he had said enough. He would keep a watchful eye with Amy and avoid unwanted concern.

As he leaned over to switch off the lamp, the bulb flickered several times. Instinctively, he looked around the room but there was no one there. Pausing for a moment, he heard Grandad Bernie cough downstairs and, relaxing again, he switched off the lamp and drifted into a deep sleep.

The next morning, Fyn and Amy rushed downstairs earlier than they would have on any other day.

'Calm down!' said Grandad Bernie. 'I can't control time! The rescue centre opens in ten minutes. I'll call them when someone is able to answer the phone!'

They begrudgingly got the message and went to sit in the living room.

A short while later they looked up expectantly as Grandad Bernie came in to see them.

'We can go and get him in an hour. In the meantime, let's get things ready.'

In high spirits, Fyn and Amy fetched a large, old rabbit hutch from the shed and cleaned it up, adding straw and a fresh blanket.

By the time they arrived at the rescue centre, Grandad Bernie was doing his best to remind them the fox would need space. 'We can't let it become too used to people,' he said again as they entered reception.

One of the animal welfare officers guided them into a small office with posters of cats, dogs, and guinea pigs dotted all over the walls among various thank you cards. She explained what they needed to know and took them through to the shelter area.

Fyn spotted the fox right away.

He was curled up in a blanket and appeared to be much better. Rather than shying away, he sniffed the air, tilting his head to watch them all.

'He's very cute,' said the officer, 'and quite a character.'

'He's so perfect,' said Amy. 'We have to give him a name.'

'Some of the team here have been calling him Henry.'

'Henry?' said Amy. 'I like it but...'

'It needs a little more,' said Fyn.

'Flame,' said Grandad Bernie, surprising them all. 'I think we should call him Henry Flame.'

CHAPTER SEVEN

Recognition

Henry Flame had beautifully bright rusty-orange fur, with brown patches on his feet and behind his ears, white around his neck, and a white tip at the end of his bushy tail. He had orange eyes with slit pupils, and a long snout which, as they soon discovered, was perfect for poking into Grandad Bernie's plant pots.

In the two days since his arrival, they had often watched from the kitchen window as he lay among the shrubs or attempted to catch grasshoppers. They tried to give him space, but it became increasingly difficult because he was naturally very inquisitive. On several occasions they had even spotted him sniffing at the back door.

'He's doing well,' said Grandad Bernie, but this made Fyn happy and sad at the same time. He knew he would miss the little fuzzball when he wasn't around, and the sooner he was better, the sooner he would have to go.

That night, Fyn and Amy were watching a classic fantasy film on the old tv while lying on the living-room floor. Fyn could hear Grandad Bernie in the kitchen, humming to the radio as he wiped down the worktops.

With no streetlights nearby and the presence of large, grey clouds filling the sky, it was particularly dark outside. No one noticed as the first drops of rain pitter-pattered on to the windows. It was only when thunder quietly rumbled that anyone stirred, and Fyn was the first.

He got up to look through the curtains, and Amy joined him at the windowsill.

The trees were gently swaying, and the rain grew steadily louder as it approached. After several minutes, a flash of lightning outlined the clouds.

Fyn's heart raced. 'Right! Shall we help in the kitchen?'

'Absolutely,' said Amy. 'I've seen this film a thousand times anyway.'

They both loved the film, but he was grateful all the same.

'Alright, you two?' asked Grandad Bernie as he tucked the tea towel into a drawer handle. 'Not feeling the weather? I thought it would be right up your street.'

The radio crackled momentarily, and the kitchen light flickered.

Fyn and Amy shared a quick glance.

Grandad Bernie's eyebrows furrowed. 'What are you up to?'

Amy kept quiet and looked down the table at a white dove-patterned fruit bowl.

Fyn was considering what to say when another flash of lightning lit up the room and an almighty crash of thunder exploded over their heads.

They all jumped. Then the power went out.

'Wooooah!' said Amy in the darkness.

'Nothing to worry about,' said Grandad Bernie. 'You two, stay here.'

He got up in the dark and went into the hallway where Fyn heard him rummaging his way around the contents of a small cupboard. There was a 'click', and a beam of light poured into the kitchen as Grandad Bernie returned with a torch. He held the beam to his face.

'I'll be right baaack,' he said in a mock creepy voice. 'I'd better check the power box in the utility room,' he added casually as he left again.

Amy moved to the kitchen window and looked out to the rabbit hutch. 'I can't see Henry Flame. I hope he's okay.'

'I'm sure he's fine,' said Fyn, his thoughts elsewhere.

'Hey,' he said, deciding to ask her what was bothering him. 'Do you think I should tell Grandad Bernie about Living-Room-Man and the weird circle of blue-and-white light?'

He could practically hear the cogs turning in her head as she fumbled her way back to the table.

'How on Earth would you start that conversation?'

'No idea,' he admitted, 'but there was a storm that night too.'

'You think it might happen again?' She shrugged. 'It doesn't feel likely.'

'I think – with Martin and everything – it's just playing on my mind.'

'What is?' asked Grandad Bernie, returning to the room and startling them both. 'The fuse has gone. I'll head out in the morning to get a new one.' He opened a drawer and took out two candles with candlesticks. 'We'll make do with these until then.'

He used a match to light them and set one on the kitchen table and one on a worktop. Then he switched off the torch and began to pour water into a pan.

Fyn decided to improvise.

'I know this will sound weird, but... I think I had a really strange dream the last time there was a big storm back home.'

'Okay,' said Grandad Bernie as he lit the gas hob with another match.

'The reason it felt so strange is because it felt like it actually happened.'

'Go on,' said Grandad Bernie. 'Tea?'

They politely declined.

'The thing is,' Fyn continued, before telling Grandad Bernie all about the events of that night and the warning about the agents – trying to keep it sounding like a dream in a similar way to how he had originally told Amy.

Grandad Bernie didn't really react as he prepared his drink, until Fyn remembered an extra detail.

'Oh, and in the dream, the man said something like "it takes all sorts to make a world". I'm not sure where I dreamt that up.'

Grandad Bernie stopped making the tea and stood with his back to them, gripping the edge of the worktop in silence.

'Are you okay?' Amy asked him.

'I... Yes...' He faced them. 'What did he say? Can you please repeat that last part again?'

'Sure,' said Fyn, feeling a little confused. 'I think it was "it takes all sorts to make a world."'

Grandad Bernie looked like the colour had drained from his face.

'Do you think you could describe him?'

Fyn hadn't expected that question.

'No, wait. I've got a better idea... Hold on.' Grandad Bernie turned off the gas, removed the pan from the hob, and took the candle from the worktop into the office opposite the living room.

'What is he doing?' Amy asked, peering around the doorframe to look after him, but he soon returned with a look of concentration on his face and a small brown photo album in his free hand.

Placing the album and the candle on the table, he sat down next to them and turned page after page until he reached a photo Fyn recognised from his parent's wedding reception.

Grandad Bernie slid the album across the table to Fyn. 'Look at this picture. What do you see?'

Fyn looked at the photo in the candlelight.

His mum beamed with delight as his dad held her in his arms. He had a rose clenched between his teeth and they were posing as if they'd just finished an energetic dance. Smiling guests surrounded them. Grandad Bernie and Grandma Frannie to their left, and his mum's parents – Fyn's Grandpop John and Granny Celia – on their right. He scanned the other faces and felt a sudden burst of shock. A man with straw-coloured hair and stubble looked back at him – the man from his living room.

Grandad Bernie closed his eyes and drew a deep breath. 'I suspected so,' he said, looking at Fyn.

'What is it?' asked Amy. 'What do you see?'

'The wedding was before Fyn was born but I believe he just recognised the man from his...' Grandad Bernie broke off slightly, '...dream.'

Fyn nodded.

Amy's jaw dropped.

Grandad Bernie continued. 'The man's name is...'

'...Scott,' Fyn finished quietly.

'Yes, that's right. Scott Triggs. You do remember a little then,' Grandad Bernie said with a smile. 'Scott and your father were best friends for as long as I can remember. Scott was best man at the wedding. He was also the other person to go missing eight years ago when your father disappeared.'

Fyn was dumbstruck. How had he not realised it before? True – he hadn't looked at the wedding photos for years, but it was absolutely Scott he had seen. He felt astounded. 'I don't think it was a dream, Grandad.'

'I'd be very much surprised if it were,' he replied quite calmly, surprising them again. 'On its own, that phrase of Scott's might not be all that special, but he was known for it. He used to say it all the time.'

'But why would you think it wasn't a dream?' Amy asked.

'Because it isn't the first time I've heard Fyn talk like that. Now with the added detail, it feels it might be something more.'

'What do you mean?' Fyn asked. 'I haven't said anything like this before, have I?'

'Just once as far as I know. I'm not surprised you don't remember.'

'When?' asked Fyn.

'About a year after you lost your father,' Grandad Bernie replied. 'You and your mother came to stay with me. You had a nightmare. We calmed you down and the next morning we all shrugged it off.'

Fyn racked his brains but had no idea what Grandad Bernie was talking about. 'What did I say?' he asked.

'You told us you had seen your father surrounded by scary light at the end of your bed. We told you it was a nightmare and to forget about it.'

Goosebumps rushed across Fyn's body. 'But surely that can't have been the same thing? I mean, why wouldn't he have come back?'

'I'm afraid I don't know. Your mother and I thought it was your way of processing things – part of the trauma of losing him. Now I find myself wondering if it was more than the bad dream we'd believed it to be. What if your father was somehow trying to contact you?'

Fyn gulped. How could this be real? 'Do you... Do you think wherever Scott is, that Dad might be with him?'

'Maybe.'

Lost for words, Fyn allowed everything to wash over him as the candle flame danced and rain continued to pour outside. Finally, he had something concrete, some link which might help lead them to understanding why his dad had left and where he had been. If only he could tell his mum.

'I'm sorry, Fyn,' said Grandad Bernie. 'I honestly thought you were going through a form of grief like the rest of us.' His eyes looked watery. 'I didn't think to believe Daniel – your father – may have really tried to contact you.'

'Just to be clear,' said Amy, 'I'm now completely on board.'

Fyn looked at them both and smiled. 'Thanks,' he said to Amy, 'and Grandad – it's not your fault. Maybe it was a dream, both that time and the time with Scott.' Even as he said it, he knew it wasn't true.

'Except,' said Amy, 'don't forget about Martin.'

'What about Martin?' asked Grandad Bernie. 'What has he got to do with all of this?'

She looked at Fyn pressingly and he nodded for her to continue.

'He knew Fyn's name.'

'*What?*' Grandad Bernie stood up and accidentally knocked the table. The candle wobbled, rocking their shadows on the walls. 'Why didn't you tell me? Do you not realise how serious this is?' He looked away for a moment, composed himself, and sat down again.

Fyn hadn't expected him to take the news well, but he didn't count on feeling so bad about it. 'I'm sorry. I didn't know what was happening. I didn't want to scare anyone.'

Grandad Bernie shook his head. 'I understand,' he said eventually, 'but we should have been more alert, and we would have been if I had known more. We'll have to think this through. Is there anything else you haven't told me?'

Feeling he owed it to his Grandad to explain the rest, Fyn filled in the gaps on what Martin had said in the woods.

'He told you to stay away from Scott?' Grandad Bernie asked.

'I think that's what he meant,' Fyn replied, 'and I guess he could be an agent.'

Grandad Bernie held steadily to the edge of the table. 'I'd definitely trust Scott over a stranger with a wild dog.'

'That's what *I* said,' said Amy.

Grandad Bernie stood up again. 'If there's a chance Scott might come back, we'll be prepared, and if he can't get to us through that circle thing, maybe we can try and get to him. Now listen, you two. It's late and there's a lot to work out. I think we all need a good kip – unless you have anything else to add?' He gave them both a stern look.

'No,' said Fyn, grateful to have it all out in the open. 'I can't believe we might have a way of contacting Dad.'

'*I* can't believe Grandad Bernie might be up for travelling through some kind of tear in reality!' said Amy in awe.

'*If* that's what it is,' said Grandad Bernie, passing them each a candle and picking up the torch. 'We'll be prepared, but we mustn't get our hopes up too high. Now come on. Time for bed.'

CHAPTER EIGHT

Trouble Comes Knocking

Fyn expected a buzz of excitement when he went into the kitchen the following morning. Instead, he found Grandad Bernie sipping coffee with a serious look about him and Amy looking miserable.

'What's happened?' Fyn asked.

Grandad Bernie sighed, but it was Amy who replied.

'Henry Flame's gone,' she said, looking up at him.

'What?' Fyn asked. 'When? How?'

'I went out to put some food down for him this morning, and he just wasn't there,' she replied.

'The garden gate might have blown open in the night,' said Grandad Bernie. 'We think the weather scared him off.'

Fyn slumped against the kitchen side. 'Oh.'

'I know, right?' said Amy, lowering her face to rest it on the table.

Fyn walked over to the window, hoping maybe it was a joke, but Henry Flame was nowhere to be seen. This was definitely not how he had expected the day to start. He wandered over to the toaster and put some bread in it before remembering there was no electricity.

'I did that too,' said Amy.

'Helpful,' he replied, shaking his head.

'I'll head to the village soon and get it sorted,' said Grandad Bernie. 'The grill still works if you light the gas.'

Fyn sat next to them and buried his head in his hands.

'It's probably for the best – Henry Flame leaving,' said Grandad Bernie.

'Why?' Fyn asked, looking at him.

'If there's even the slightest chance of us heading off to wherever Scott is,' Grandad Bernie replied, 'we're going to need some time to plan. We can't rightly go away and leave a fox trapped in the garden, even if he is healing up nicely.'

'I'll miss him though,' said Fyn.

'Me too,' said Grandad Bernie.

'Me three,' said Amy.

'Maybe we'll see him again,' Fyn suggested, 'and... well ... *maybe* Dad and Scott will find a way to come to us.'

'Perhaps,' said Grandad Bernie, 'although I wouldn't count on it. I'm sure they'd be here already if they could be. It might be down to us.'

'We're with you,' said Amy, her face still pressed against the table. 'Aren't we, Fyn?'

'Of course!' he replied, a little frustrated she felt the need to ask. 'I'd go on my own if I had to.'

'You're not going anywhere without me!' she retorted, looking up quickly.

'Alright you two,' said Grandad Bernie. 'I think we're all in agreement that no one is being left behind.'

'Apart from Henry Flame,' said Amy miserably.

Fyn always loved staying at Grandad Bernie's, but, even with the hope that his dad may be alive, he couldn't help feeling a little deflated now that Henry Flame was gone.

He had grown accustomed to seeing the orange fuzzball hopping about the garden and wasn't sure how long it would take until he stopped expecting to see him there.

Grandad Bernie came in the front door, placing some bags on the floor. 'I've got fuses, plus a bunch of other stuff in case we go, well, anywhere. George Sparrow – the man who runs Sparrow's Bric-a-Brac shop with his wife Marlene

– said they had a visit from a police officer doing the rounds. At least we know they're taking the news about Martin seriously.'

'I guess that's something,' said Fyn.

'Or better,' said Grandad Bernie. 'Come on now, cheer up. Things will be okay.' Then he went and replaced the blown fuse before they sat to discuss their plans.

Fyn and Amy agreed to trust that Henry Flame must have been better for him to have been able to leave them, so the excitement of trying to find Fyn's dad started sinking in.

'I think we should pack everything right away!' declared Amy. 'We have no idea when anything might happen.'

Fyn nodded. 'I can't believe we're really thinking about this. I mean, I want to but … wow!'

They packed their things, enjoyed spinach-and-ricotta cannelloni with garlic dough balls and salad for dinner, then settled at the kitchen table to distract themselves with a jigsaw puzzle.

Fyn had found it when looking under the bed in his room. He thought it seemed appropriate. It was a large picture of woodland animals including a family of foxes.

He and Amy focused on the edges as Grandad Bernie grouped pieces together by colour.

Fyn was just about to stop Amy from attempting to attach a badger's backside to a rabbit's face, when there were two loud knocks at the door.

'Stay here you two,' said Grandad Bernie, 'and keep quiet just in case'. He stood up and left the kitchen, pulling the door to on the way.

Quickly and quietly, Fyn and Amy got up and snuck over to listen.

Grandad Bernie opened the front door.

'Good evening,' came the voice of a smart-sounding man. 'I'm PC Smith from the local station. I'm just doing the rounds to ensure everyone is aware of...'

Amy turned to Fyn and whispered, 'Did you hear that? It's the police! They might have more news on Martin!'

'I know,' Fyn whispered back. 'Better listen then!'

She gave him a cheeky shove, but he ignored it. He wasn't sure why, but something felt off.

'Stay here. I'm going in!' He stepped through the kitchen archway into the living room. Moving silently towards the front windows, he glanced back and saw Amy looking dumbstruck at him.

Grandad Bernie was in deep conversation at the front door. 'Thank you, but it's okay. I'm the person who reported Martin in the first place. It was my grandson who spotted him nearby.'

'Ah yes, I apologise,' said the policeman smoothly. 'I've been doing the rounds all day and should have realised I'd reached your residence. Of course you're right. If you wouldn't mind me coming in, it would be good to review the details in case you've remembered something new.'

Fyn had now climbed onto the sofa and was trying to peek through the net curtains.

Amy tiptoed across the living room and stood at the door by the hallway to listen in better.

'Not right now, thank you,' Grandad Bernie declined. 'It's not the best time. Dinner's nearly done and there's nothing more to report. I already advised everything over the phone.'

Fyn looked at Amy in surprise. *Did he just ... lie to the police?*

'It would be helpful to hear it from the young man himself,' said the officer.

'I don't think so,' said Grandad Bernie. 'If anything, seeing the fox wounded in that way affected the lad and I don't want to bring it up with him again. Not tonight anyway.'

Amy gave Fyn a confused look.

He shrugged.

'Sir, I politely insist. Any additional details could aid our investigation.'

'Honestly, officer, we haven't got anything else to add. I'll speak to him on my own terms and promise to give you a call at the station first thing in the morning. I'll make sure you are fully informed, and I'll speak to Sergeant Wallis if there's any concern tonight. Now I am sorry, but I must be going. Have yourself a pleasant evening.'

Fyn heard Grandad Bernie close the front door and watched as the policeman turned around. When Fyn saw his face, he threw himself backwards off the sofa and fell hard to the floor.

'What are you doing?' hissed Amy. 'Grandad Bernie's coming!'

Fyn didn't care. He knew something hadn't been right – the voice was too familiar. It was Martin. The policeman was Martin.

CHAPTER NINE

One Way Out

A shadow crossed the window and Fyn saw Martin's face silhouetted against the net curtains, trying to look inside.

'Hide!' Fyn said, as he rolled to the base of the sofa.

A confused-looking Amy retreated behind the door and Fyn listened as Martin shuffled around outside, seeking a better view. Then Grandad Bernie walked into the living room.

Amy was so startled she jumped out from behind the door and screamed, which in turn made Grandad Bernie leap out of his slippers.

'For heaven's sake!' he exclaimed. 'What are you doing in here? And what are *you* doing on the floor?'

Fyn scrambled to his feet as the face outside disappeared. Had Martin seen them?

'The policeman, Grandad! It was Martin!'

'*What?*' shrieked Amy.

'I thought he might be,' sighed Grandad Bernie as he walked over to the window. 'He's off now though.'

Fyn was stunned. 'How did you know?'

'I didn't at first or I wouldn't have said you were here. I've lived in this village for years and it's only got a small police station. He's not one of the officers they send out for this sort of thing. I should have put two and two together. He didn't show any ID. He didn't realise we're the house that reported him, and he didn't arrive in a car. No officer is going to do the rounds without a car, especially with the weather as it is. I'm surprised George – from Sparrow's Bric-a-Brac – didn't pick up on it.'

'Maybe he was visited by a genuine officer,' said Fyn.

'Perhaps,' Grandad Bernie agreed.

'Should we call the real police then?' Amy asked. 'I mean now Martin knows Fyn is here?'

'I think so,' said Grandad Bernie. 'Better to play it safe. With any luck he'll expect me to call them anyway and might keep away. Especially as I mentioned the Sergeant.'

Fyn didn't like it. Why was Martin trying to find him, and why would he go through such lengths to do it? If Martin was an agent, why would he need to impersonate the police?

Later, after Fyn, Amy, and Grandad Bernie had explained to two genuine police officers about Martin's visit and been reassured the officers would up their local patrols, a fine, drizzly rain began to fall.

'Do you think it's okay that we told them Martin knew Fyn?' Amy asked as she zipped up her hoodie.

'It's always best to tell the truth,' Grandad Bernie replied, 'especially to the police – or at least to the real ones.'

'What about Scott?' asked Fyn. 'We didn't mention him.' He couldn't help but wonder if Grandad Bernie had left that part out on purpose.

'I didn't think we needed to,' he replied. 'It's just our guess really and it might not be related. I'd rather they focus on the main issue.'

'Which is?' Fyn asked.

'Martin knows more about you than he should.'

Fyn gulped. Grandad Bernie had a point. 'I hope it's all sorted before my mum comes home.'

'Me too,' said Grandad Bernie. 'It should be much easier to explain that way.'

They locked the windows and doors, put their backpacks by the kitchen table, and settled down for the night.

Fyn sat bolt upright. What had woken him? It sounded like a bang. In his dream it was a door flying open, but it felt as though he really heard it. The bedroom was dark, and the rain was heavier than the night before. He heard a gentle knock.

'Fyn, it's me.' Amy's muffled voice came quietly through the door. 'Are you awake?'

'Come in,' he replied.

She opened the door and stepped into the room as he flicked on the lamp.

'Did you knock a moment ago?' he asked.

'You mean just before I walked in?'

'No. A bit before that.'

'Not me...' She looked at him with interest.

'How come you're up?' he asked.

'I couldn't sleep. This storm is amazing but it's kind of freaking me out a bit. There's so much going on right now.'

'I know what you mean,' he said. 'I'm just trying to act normal.'

'How can we act normal with all that's happening?'

He shrugged. 'I don't know.'

She sat gently on the end of the bed as a double flash of lightning brightened the walls. 'I can't stop wondering if Martin will come back. What if he brings his dog? I guess that's one good thing about Henry Flame not being here – he can't be hurt by it again.'

'We can't think like that,' said Fyn, but, when she looked less than convinced, he added, 'I'm not saying it's easy. I just don't know what else we can do. I'd welcome any ideas you might have.'

'I'm ready to swing the lamp by my bed if I need to,' she said straight-faced.

He grinned. 'Here's hoping it doesn't come to that. We just need to relax. Shall we go sit in the kitchen? We won't have to be so quiet there.'

Amy nodded. 'Good idea.'

They snuck downstairs in the dark, trying not to wake Grandad Bernie.

In the hallway, just past the ticking grandfather clock, a shadow moved across the wall. The kitchen light was on.

Before Fyn could process what was happening, a man stepped out ahead of them.

'AHHHH!' All three of them shouted.

The hallway light switched on. It was Grandad Bernie.

'For goodness' sake! What are you two doing up at this time? That's the second time you've made me jump like that!'

'Made *you* jump? What about us?' Fyn shook his head in dismay. His heart was pounding.

Amy laughed. 'That's just the distraction I needed! Thanks!'

Grandad Bernie frowned. 'So happy to help. I see you couldn't sleep either. Fancy a hot drink?'

Fyn followed the others into the kitchen and sat at the table. The kitchen light flickered.

'Why do the lights always do that, Grandad?' he asked.

'It's probably just the weather,' he replied. 'I can't say I've taken much notice to be honest.'

It flickered again.

'I noticed *that* time. Don't forget we're not in a big town out here.'

Another light flashed across the wall, but this time it wasn't from the bulb or lightning.

Excitement rushed through Fyn. Was this the moment they'd been hoping for?

As if in answer, blue-and-white light began to flash furiously all around them. It was coming through the archway from the living room.

He looked at Grandad Bernie and Amy.

Amy looked like she'd seen a ghost.

Grandad Bernie stood frozen with the teaspoon in his hand.

Fyn jumped up from the table, passing them their backpacks before grabbing his own. Then he sped through the archway.

A large circle of crackling blue-and-white light hung in the middle of the air. Scott's face was in the centre.

'Fyn! Thank goodness. I'm sorry about last time. Oh!'

Grandad Bernie and Amy joined Fyn at his side.

'I... I can't believe it!' Scott said. 'Bernie? Is that really you?'

Grandad Bernie stood still, his eyes wide.

'It's him!' said Fyn. 'Scott, what are you doing here? Where are you?'

'I'll tell you all about it, but I—'

BOOM!

The back door flew open.

Martin ran into the kitchen, his thin, wet hair matted to his head and his eyes searching wildly.

Samson ran in afterwards, barking behind him.

They both looked around frantically until they spotted everyone else in the next room.

Martin's eyes darted back and forth between Fyn and the shimmering circle of light.

'Stay away from that!'

Samson growled viciously.

'Quickly!' called Scott. 'There's no choice! You need to climb through!'

Fyn looked at the others.

'Go!' shouted Grandad Bernie.

'Stop!' screamed Martin, running at them with Samson who took the lead and closed in on Amy.

Out of nowhere, a small orange blur dived through the open back door and into the kitchen, where it sunk its teeth into one of Samson's hind legs. The dog yelped in pain, and a bewildered Martin stopped in his tracks to see the cause of the disruption.

'Henry!' called Amy. 'Come on, Henry!'

Rain pelted into the kitchen as the wind blew the back door rapidly to and fro. Thunder crashed above them.

Before Samson could recover, Henry Flame charged past him, but Martin started running at them again.

With no time to hesitate, Fyn reached out for Scott and instantly felt himself pulled into the circle, narrowly seeing Grandad Bernie and Amy reaching out behind him. He only just caught sight of Henry Flame leaping after them.

He felt as though every fibre of his being was pulsing and shaking so quickly he could be pulled apart. Like a twisting rubber band, he was stretched and compressed all at once, surrounded by images and light as he headed into the unknown.

CHAPTER TEN

Far from Home

Fyn watched as glimpses of Grandad Bernie, Amy, and Henry Flame came towards him, then stretched away.

Surrounding them was Grandad Bernie's living room and something else. Mixed in with the familiar was the unfamiliar: tropical-looking trees, the night sky, and Scott who he saw in snippets among the rest.

Everything snapped into place.

Fyn fell onto his knees and Grandad Bernie, Amy, and Henry Flame fell on top of him in a heap of moans, groans, and backpacks.

Henry Flame shook himself off and ran into the darkness.

'Wait!' Fyn tried to call, but instead he gagged with the urge to throw up. He felt like he'd been freefalling on a rollercoaster.

Scott bent down and tapped a button on a strange device.

As Fyn looked up, he saw Martin's face contort with rage and frustration as the circle of blue-and-white light closed in on itself seconds before he could reach it.

Scott helped them to their feet. 'Don't worry. You'll feel better soon, but we have to move. Amy is that you?'

She nodded while holding her hand over her mouth.

Fyn steadied himself against a tree, trying not to fall over. Wherever they were, it was humid. Traces of moonlight outlined vine covered trees all around them. Enormous palm leaves towered high above.

'Where are we? Are we ... in a jungle?' he asked, holding his stomach.

'Far from home,' said Scott. 'Before we go, are any of you carrying anything that uses power? Maybe something with batteries?' He picked up the strange device and carefully placed it into a sling across his back.

Fyn and Amy had left their phones back at the house, but along with Grandad Bernie they opened their bags and pulled out their torches.

'You must *never* use them,' Scott warned, 'or anything with power like that here. It's strictly forbidden – for the most part at least. In fact, it would be better if you take the batteries out.'

They did as he suggested.

'I know it sounds strange but the use of power like that is monitored here. Only the agents are allowed to use it and they trace unauthorised usage. They'll no doubt be on their way to see what caused the reading from this.' He pointed to the sling on his back.

Amy looked anxiously into the wilderness. 'What about Henry Flame?'

'Henry Flame?' asked Scott.

'A rather extraordinary fox,' said Grandad Bernie while holding his stomach. 'He came with us through...' He waved an arm in the air at the spot where they'd arrived.

'I'm sorry, but we can't stay to look,' said Scott. 'He could be anywhere by now. There's plenty out here to keep him going though.'

'Can't we just try and call him?' asked Fyn.

'Not without drawing more attention to ourselves,' Scott replied. 'I'm sure he'll be fine.'

Fyn and Amy looked to Grandad Bernie.

'He'll be okay,' he reassured them. 'In fact, I wouldn't be at all surprised if he finds us before we find him.'

'I'm sorry,' said Scott again. 'Now, be on your guard, stay close, and move as quietly as you can.'

'Before we go,' said Grandad Bernie. 'Is Daniel here?'

'He made it here...' said Scott.

Fyn felt relief flow through him.

'...but,' Scott continued, 'I haven't seen him for some time. It's part of the reason I've been concerned for Fyn's safety. I'm excited to catch up, but we must move, and it's best to stay quiet. Agents won't be far away. We can talk later.'

It wasn't exactly the news Fyn had been hoping for, but he bristled with excitement from the confirmation that his dad had been here. Even if everything else seemed confusing, at least they were closer now.

Ignoring that they were still wearing their nightclothes, they put on the walking trainers they had in their bags. Fyn didn't really mind his red shorts and white t-shirt anyway, and he was pretty sure Grandad Bernie wouldn't mind his own colourful checked pyjamas. On the other hand, Amy's night top and bottoms were covered in bright elephants, and her fluffy pink socks looked like mini cats – whiskers included. Fyn smiled, knowing she would be fine.

They followed Scott in silence as he looked up and all around, carefully moving from tree to tree, always keeping to the shadows and out of direct moonlight.

The ground was uneven – smooth and slippery in some places, rough and jagged in others. Fyn nearly tripped several times, especially as he kept watch for Henry Flame.

He had so many questions and kept flitting between excitement and uncertainty. Where were they and how had they travelled here? Where was his dad and why did his disappearance mean Fyn could be in danger? Would Martin be waiting for them when they got back?

Assuming we can *get back...* Fyn thought, making him feel light-headed. He stopped walking.

Grandad Bernie rested his hand on Fyn's arm. 'You okay, short stuff?'

Fyn nodded gratefully and they continued on.

After a while, his thoughts turned to where they were going and when they would be able to rest. He staggered as he walked, tiredness catching up to him, but he was determined to stay awake. If possible, he wanted answers.

Wind lightly whistled through the upper layers of the trees. Insects and creatures clicked, chirped, and croaked.

'Don't move!' Scott said, startling them to a stop.

Fyn was about to ask what was happening when Scott spoke again.

'This way!' He gestured for them to follow him to an enormous tree, ducking under its twisted roots which were raised high above the ground.

As Fyn and the others took cover with him, a low humming sound began to fill the sky.

Three blue lights were flying towards them, leaving a trail in Fyn's vision. When they stopped, they hovered overhead.

Trying for a better view, he moved his face closer to the roots. They appeared to be vehicles, but unlike any he'd seen before, and they were covered in a series of glowing neon-blue pipework. It was hard to be certain, but it looked like there was a person seated on each of them.

Without warning they shot beams of light to the ground and lit up the area around them. Fyn backed away from the gaps in the roots, shielding his eyes and trying to bury himself deeper out of sight, further into the undergrowth. Then he waited nervously.

'What are they?' he whispered, but no one replied.

Scott held a finger to his lips.

The vehicles and their lights moved as smoothly and sporadically as water skaters on a pond, searching for something in the darkness. Then as quickly as they came, they were gone. The only sounds remaining were those of the jungle and the whistling wind.

Scott brushed himself off as he stood up, then he helped Grandad Bernie to his feet. 'We should be okay for now, but we can't be too careful.'

'What were those things?' asked Amy.

Scott's tone was grim. 'Soarers,' he replied, 'and … agents.'

There was no point in asking anything else. He had already turned and started walking again.

Chapter Eleven

Eromlos

They settled for the night on a ridge partway down a cliff that overlooked the sea.

Fyn had been glad to hear the waves crashing below and was calmed by the white of the moonlight on the water, but he was also intrigued by the towering stones at the cliff edge which were inscribed with strange markings.

'Ancient language,' was the only explanation Scott had given as they passed them on their way down.

Amy had struggled a bit due to her fear of heights, so Fyn had walked on the side closest to the sea to help her. It wasn't too steep. Certainly not as bad as waiting even longer for answers, but Grandad Bernie made them rest until morning so they could discuss things with fresh minds.

With the sun now rising and a cool breeze blowing in from the sea, Fyn and the others settled around Scott. He was laying out supplies that had been tied to the trunk of a fallen tree for those in need. He handed them sultanas the size of fists with some dried meat. Then he passed them each a wooden cup with water he'd collected earlier.

'I'm so glad to see you all, although I never imagined I'd see the day you'd be here!' He shook his head. 'I'd love to hear all about your lives and how you are, but you must be desperate to know what's happening. The only challenge is knowing where to begin.'

'If you don't mind,' said Grandad Bernie, 'where is Daniel?'

Scott sighed. 'That's sort of the problem ... I don't know. He's been missing for a few months. It's one of the reasons I contacted Fyn.'

'Me?' said Fyn uncertainly. 'I have no idea where he is. I've never known...'

'Sorry,' said Scott. 'That's not what I meant. I knew he couldn't be with you. The use of world windows – like the thing you travelled through to get here – is absolutely forbidden. Even more than normal technology. Daniel would never put you or others at risk by using one.'

'So, he never used one? A world window I mean,' Fyn asked, thinking about what Grandad Bernie had said and wondering if it was his dad he had seen when he was younger or if it had been a nightmare. 'It's just ... we think he may have tried when I was little.'

'Wow,' said Scott. 'Good memory. You're right. He did try once, but only to communicate. Not to travel.'

'What happened?' Fyn asked. 'Why didn't he try again?'

Scott shifted a bit. 'You mustn't blame yourself,' he said, instantly making Fyn uncomfortable. 'He knew he was taking a risk when he tried that one time. I know you were only young, but apparently you really panicked and couldn't be consoled. He ended up feeling he'd done worse by trying to contact you, so he put his efforts into his work instead, hoping we'd find a better way.'

Fyn didn't feel better knowing this. If he hadn't reacted badly, his dad might have stuck around longer or tried again.

'Why did *you* use a world window?' Amy asked. 'If you knew the risks, I mean.'

'It's a valid question,' said Scott, 'and I'd never normally mess with things in this way. I thought Fyn could be in danger.'

'From what?' Grandad Bernie asked.

'The agents,' Scott replied. 'If they ever learn about Fyn, they could use him to get to his father.'

Grandad Bernie frowned. 'Why would they do that?'

'He's a brilliant scientist. We mostly keep ourselves to ourselves here, but if the agents have got to him and learned of his skills … they'd find him extremely useful. Who knows what they'd do to learn more?'

'Aren't you a scientist too?' Amy asked.

He nodded. 'Yes, and I expect I'd be just as at risk if they found out about me…'

No one spoke for a short time. The waves continued to wash rhythmically on to the shore below.

Fyn turned the questions around in his head. There was so much to consider. 'Who are the agents?' he asked eventually.

'They could be anyone,' Scott replied. 'Here they call themselves guardians, but don't be fooled – they only protect themselves. They were the ones flying the soarers last night, and they're the ones who monitor the use of energy. There are pros and cons to this place. If there's anything for certain – it's always best to keep out of trouble with the agents.'

Fyn began to feel light-headed again.

Amy rested one of her feet against his. 'Scott, would you… I mean, if it's alright, could you please tell us your story?'

'Of course,' he replied. 'I think it's a good idea.'

Fyn, Amy, and Grandad Bernie leaned in closer to listen.

Scott cleared his throat. 'As you may or may not know, eight years ago, Daniel and I were on an expedition in the Himalayas. It was a joint research trip. It feels like a lifetime ago now. Anyway, it was going well. For some it was geological, to understand more about the formation of the mountains. For others it was to observe the wildlife. For your father and I,' he looked at Fyn, 'it was to try to understand energy processes in the environment. We were out recording data one day and a storm picked up around us.'

Fyn and Amy glanced at each other.

Another storm.

'We were very open to the elements and things soon got out of hand. The wind was blowing us all over the place and we didn't have much to keep us tethered to the ground. To try and stabilise us, I hammered my walking pole into some rocks. I wanted to give us something to hold on to, but it didn't work.'

'Why not?' asked Fyn.

'We didn't realise how delicate the ground was. We were standing on the roof of a large underground cavern. I'm surprised we were able to walk on it at all. As I forced my walking pole into it, it gave way beneath our feet.'

Fyn could picture every moment in his mind. His dad falling, and the fear on his face as he tried to understand what was happening. Had his life flashed before his eyes? Finally, things were beginning to make sense.

'It was terrifying,' said Scott. 'Daniel and I have talked about it a lot since then. We thought we were done for!'

'How *did* you survive?' asked Grandad Bernie.

'That's where it gets really interesting,' said Scott. 'Even though it felt like forever, I don't think we can have fallen for long. A river flowed through the cavern, and while it hurt to land in it, it likely saved our lives. Somehow, I kept hold of my walking pole and I wedged it into the riverbank. Daniel grabbed hold of me. We were hanging on for our lives without knowing where we'd end up if we let go. Then everything changed.'

'How?' asked Fyn, Amy, and Grandad Bernie all at once.

'It's crazy,' said Scott, 'because I'd never have expected you to believe it before, but maybe you will now you've seen it for yourselves. We were hanging on with everything we had when, out of nowhere, a world window opened a few metres downstream. I must have swallowed a litre of water in shock. Without meaning to, I let go of the pole, and Daniel let go of me. The river swept us away but instead of taking us wherever it usually flowed, it took us directly through the world window. We wound up here, or at least in this world.'

'In this world?' echoed Fyn, more to himself than anyone else but loud enough for the others to hear. 'Where are we?' He knew they were nowhere near home, but in another world completely... How could that be?

Scott looked to the ground before meeting their gaze. 'It won't be easy to take in, but I promise it's the truth. We're not on *our* Earth. We're on another version of Earth. This one is called Eromlos.'

Stunned silence followed his words and Fyn pinched himself absentmindedly to see if he would wake up. He didn't. This was happening.

'At first your father and I couldn't believe it either. I wish I could buffer it for you but it's going to take time to comprehend. Simply put, our Earth is in one of many universes and right now we're on the Earth in another one.'

Multiverses are real, thought Fyn in bewilderment. No wonder there had been no sign of his dad back home. His palms began to sweat through excitement or nerves.

Scott sat patiently as they processed the initial shock.

Amy buried her head in her hands, and Grandad Bernie stared at the cliff face.

Fyn felt like his thoughts were stuck on shuffle. He didn't know which to settle on. It was like all the stories, games, and films he'd ever seen about parallel worlds now had some truth to them.

'This might sound like an obvious question,' Grandad Bernie said eventually, 'but how can you be sure what you're saying is correct? How can you know something like that?'

'I really do understand where you're coming from,' Scott replied, 'but I've been here for a long time and asked myself every question you can imagine. Am I on the other side of the world? Am I hallucinating? Have I lost my mind? Maybe I'm even in a coma and dreaming somewhere, but you saw what happened back there. Have you ever seen things like those on our Earth?'

'The ... the soarers?' Fyn asked.

Scott nodded. 'That's before we even think about the world windows.'

Grandad Bernie fell silent again.

'Listen,' said Scott. 'We're less than half a day from home.'

The word struck in Fyn's mind. *Home*.

'Let things sink in as we go. They'll be time for more talk later.'

With that, they packed up and trekked on. The jungle was louder in the day so, although they remained quiet, Scott wasn't as concerned about their noise. Still, they stuck to the cover of the trees. 'Agents rest for no one,' he said.

Fyn couldn't help thinking they'd stand out anyway – especially in their pyjamas.

They stopped occasionally to catch their breath, and on one break Scott introduced them to 'yellow sleeves': the equivalent of arm-length bananas which tasted like candy floss, and 'purple pods': delicate, berry-like fruits contained in a tough exterior. The latter grossed Fyn and Amy out a bit. They needed to be squeezed until the gooey fruit erupted with an uncomfortably satisfying pop.

With so much to see and even more to think about, the journey didn't feel like it took long at all, and when they found themselves in a clearing at the bottom of a slope covered in wooden buildings, Scott turned to them and smiled.

'Welcome to Homehill.'

CHAPTER TWELVE

Ancient History

Scott led the way up and into Homehill on a path of sun-bleached stones and shells. The buildings they passed were more than standard huts, but not quite houses as Fyn knew them. They looked well crafted and maintained, but also basic and open to the elements. Each was raised above the ground on sturdy beams of wood and had steps leading up to a porch, but their doorways had no doors and instead were covered with sheets of cloth.

Everyone Fyn saw looked genuinely happy. Younger children laughed as they played, whether running and rolling around or skipping with ropes made of vines. A group about his age were carving arrows and firing them from bows into heavily marked tree trunks. Adults chatted in the shade – some preparing fruit or sewing clothes and others chopping wood or carrying baskets with wide lids. Many smiled and waved at Scott, and a few looked curiously, as though trying to figure out who he had brought with him.

There were no cables or pylons in sight. No satellite dishes. No aerials. No streetlights or mobile phones, but even if the so-called guardians didn't allow technology here, it didn't seem to dampen the spirit of the villagers.

Fyn found it quite unusual to see so many people outside enjoying each other's company. It was different to back home where his neighbours kept themselves to themselves. What if his dad had been happy here? Scott didn't exactly seem unhappy himself.

They stopped about three quarters of the way up the hill where Scott pointed to one of the homes. 'This is where I live and ... err ... I have a little surprise for you.'

As Fyn wondered what he could mean, Scott led them up the porch to the sheet overhanging the doorway. In the middle of it was a symbol of a star, surrounded by a ring of five waves peaking towards it. The image was contained within a green circle. Scott moved the sheet back and an eruption of noise greeted them.

Two young boys ran to hug Scott around the legs. A woman carrying a little girl followed.

'Hi!' he said happily to the children, 'and hello, love,' he added softly to the woman as she greeted him with a kiss.

'I'm glad you're okay,' she replied, looking uncertainly from Scott to Fyn and the others. 'You are okay, aren't you?'

'I'm fine,' he replied.

Fyn shuffled his feet awkwardly. How had he not considered Scott could have a new life after so many years? What if it was the same for his dad? He looked away, unsure what to feel, and spotted Amy who silently mouthed the word 'wow' to him.

'I realise it must be a shock,' Scott said to Fyn, Amy, and Grandad Bernie, 'but I didn't have any family left on Earth, so settling on Eromlos wasn't really a problem for me.'

'It's certainly a surprise but ... congratulations!' said Grandad Bernie, embracing him and patting him on the back.

'Scott?' the woman asked, moving closer to him.

'Nothing to worry about,' he reassured her. 'The night didn't go as planned, but wait until you find out who I have with me.' He turned back to Fyn, Amy, and Grandad Bernie. 'This is Daniel's father, Bernie...'

The woman gasped.

'...Daniel's son, Fyn,' Scott continued, 'and their close family friend, Amy – the daughter of Mark and Chloe who I've told you about.'

She stared at them all, wide-eyed and lost for words.

'I know,' he smiled. 'And to our new arrivals, this is my beautiful partner, Marina, our eldest son Lance who is six, our second son Lucas who is four, and little Rosie here, who is one.' His pride was obvious as he lifted the young girl from Marina's arms and held her close.

Rosie stared at him with her big brown eyes and laughed cheekily.

'This is amazing,' said Marina. 'Please, everyone, come in. Our home is your home.' She gestured to some stools topped with plump pillows at the edges of the room.

Fyn glanced around at handmade shelves decorated with patterned stones and knick-knacks, wooden toys, and colourful fabrics. The more he looked at the home comforts, the more a dread-like sensation began to creep through him. Exactly how much *had* changed in eight years? He was happy for Scott, but what if his dad had found a new family too? He felt like the air was leaving the room.

'You look as if you're carrying too much on your mind,' said Marina. 'Please, take a seat.'

He felt her hands on his shoulders as she ushered him to a stool.

'There's nothing to worry about,' Scott said softly. 'Your father hasn't set up home like I have. I mean, he has a place here, but he always held out for you.'

'I... Thanks,' said Fyn, relaxing a little.

'No problem,' Scott replied knowingly. 'Now come on. Make yourselves at home.'

'I'll get drinks,' said Marina, hurrying to a big bamboo jug on a table at the other end of the room.

Grandad Bernie and Amy sat next to Fyn, who realised that they, too, seemed a little shell-shocked. They looked at each other, to their surroundings, then back to each other again, no one quite seeming to know what to say.

Fyn observed Scott and his family.

Scott hadn't really changed from the photograph in Grandad Bernie's album. His straw-coloured hair and stubble now had flecks of grey; otherwise, he was the same trimly shaped man as before.

The youngest of the boys, Lucas, clearly took after him with his blond hair and green eyes, but Lance and Rosie had the dark brown hair and eyes of their mum.

Marina poured them some water and carried it over. 'We had a visit from the guardians this morning. Some of the villagers said they spotted soarers in the sky last night. I was concerned.'

Scott tensed at the mention of the guardians. 'What did they want?'

'We're fine,' said Marina dismissively. 'They stopped by every home in the village. They said they were checking on a disruption but wouldn't say what it was. I didn't know what to think...'

Fyn shifted on the stool. The agents really were a threat. At least back home they had the police. Here, it seemed the agents *were* the police. His mind flicked back to Martin and his impersonation.

Scott looked at Lance and Lucas who were playing in a corner. 'Boys, could you please go up and see Rogan? Tell him I'm back and I've brought guests from my old home. He'll know what I mean. Tell him we'd like to see him later. You can play outside on the way back.'

With an excited look at each other, they zoomed out, and Fyn watched through the window as they ran up the hill.

Scott removed the sling from his back while balancing Rosie, and gently placed it on a table. 'You know recently I've been trying to watch out for Fyn,' he said to Marina.

'You were worried for him.'

'Exactly.' He turned to Fyn. 'Rogan is our village leader. Your father and I have been working with him. He obtained the device in this sling long ago and I've been using it to communicate with you. Only a few in the village know about it – the same people who know guardians are agents.' He looked back to Marina. 'When I saw Fyn last night, an agent tried to attack him and the others.'

'Wait,' said Fyn, his suspicions all but confirmed. 'You mean Martin *was* an agent?'

'I believe so,' replied Scott. 'I can't think why else he would have been there.'

Fyn looked to Amy. 'This is real,' he said under his breath, the enormity of things starting to dawn on him again.

She nodded back, her jaw clamped shut.

'There was no time,' Scott continued to Marina, 'so I called them through the world window. I know I shouldn't have, but it was the only thing I could do to help. That's likely the reason the soarers came.'

'I understand,' she replied thoughtfully. 'At least they made it here okay.'

Fyn's thoughts turned to Henry Flame. Was *he* okay? Then he thought a little more. 'You said earlier that world windows are more forbidden than other technology, but why is that? Why have we never heard of them?'

Scott was about to answer, but Fyn continued.

'If you could create a world window, why didn't you come home? I know you said it's a risk, but you gave up everything.' The words sounded more like an accusation than he'd intended, but he didn't apologise. Instead, he waited like he had for what felt like his entire life and ignored the tension in the room.

Scott sat with Marina as Rosie continued to hold him. 'They know how Daniel and I got here, and that Daniel is missing,' he explained to Marina before sighing. 'It's time to fill some more gaps.'

She pursed her lips, and her eyes looked sad. 'I believe so.'

'I'll tell you what Rogan told your father and I when he first brought us to Homehill,' Scott replied to Fyn.

'Rogan's a good man, and he knows things, but even this won't give you everything you need.'

Fyn nodded. He didn't care what he found out. He just wanted to know.

Scott took a sip of his water. 'Many centuries ago, people used special gateways to travel between parallel universes. Apparently, it was quite a common thing to do. Rogan thinks back then it may have brought a sense of peace to the people, because they didn't feel as alone any more. Eventually a corrupt world crossed the line. In their quest for power, they sent ambassadors to other worlds, connecting with resources they wanted for their own, threatening whoever they needed to on the way. It was the beginning of catastrophe.'

'Out of so many worlds, how could one make such a difference?' asked Amy.

'One *person* can make a difference,' said Grandad Bernie. 'I imagine a whole world of people can make a very large difference indeed – if they set their minds to it.'

'Absolutely,' said Scott.

Fyn didn't understand how this explained anything. 'Why didn't the people argue or fight back?' he asked.

'Not everyone can,' Scott replied. 'With enough force against you, I imagine it's easy to feel backed into a corner...'

'Yes,' said Marina passionately, 'though let's not forget their strength.'

Scott smiled at her. 'I wouldn't dare.' He turned back to Fyn and the others. 'Realising the threat, many world leaders grouped together and stood united. They formed a treaty and vowed to stand against the enemy and any others which might appear in time.'

'I sense a "but" coming,' said Amy.

'A *big* "but",' said Scott.

Fyn caught Amy's eye, and for a moment they shared a smirk.

Grandad Bernie shook his head. '*Really?*'

Scott chuckled, '*But* when the enemy realised the treaty was against them, they reacted with ferocious speed. They got it wrong. Every version of Earth with a gateway was victim to a blast of devastating destruction – including their own. People must have thought it was the end. The lining between worlds was damaged and world windows generated all over the place. Worlds began to shift. Entire land masses with all their creatures were transferred from one Earth to another. Weather systems went haywire. Countless people died. Nothing was the same again.'

'It must have been terrifying,' said Marina.

Fyn heard the sincerity in her voice. He liked her. 'How did it stop?' he asked.

'The gateways were the key,' Scott replied. 'Built to handle masses of energy they survived the blasts but, with so many open and the universes so fragile, there was too much instability. All worlds agreed to dismantle their gateways and destroy evidence of their creation. Under less strain, the universes stabilised, and people learned to live as they had before. Over the course of time the stories were lost to legend.'

Rosie laughed and jolted them out of the conversation. She had noticed the elephants on Amy's pyjamas and was reaching out for them.

Scott lowered her to the floor, and she toddled over to Amy.

'Can I pick her up?' Amy asked.

'She'd like that,' said Marina, 'although she makes a good point. You'll want fresh clothes so you don't stand out as much. Where will they be staying?' she asked Scott.

'We'll check with Rogan when we see him,' he replied.

Realisation dawned on Fyn. 'I didn't think. We knew we may be coming here, but we didn't know where *here* was. I never thought about staying.'

When Scott spoke again his tone was bleak. 'Things have changed so much with your arrival... Travel between worlds really is forbidden. Your father and I didn't come home because the risks of further devastation were too great.'

Fyn gripped his knees tightly. 'Are you saying what I think you're saying?'

'It's just we don't know—'

'—if we can go home again...' Fyn interrupted as he realised the truth. Like his dad and Scott before them, they were now stuck on Eromlos.

Chapter Thirteen
At Home on Homehill

'Fyn...' started Grandad Bernie.

'I'm sorry, Grandad,' Fyn replied as he stood up, 'but I can't calm down. We knew we were trying to find my dad but what about my mum? She's been through so much already! We can't just leave her, and what about Amy's family? It's not like we left a note!'

The reality of being stuck on Eromlos hit him hard and he went from being full of thoughts to feeling like every thought had abandoned him. He sat down again in silence.

'Fyn, please...' said Grandad Bernie, but this time it was Amy who cut him off.

'Fyn is right. We said we're in this together – and we are – but did anyone really think we might not make it home?'

Grandad Bernie faltered.

'We should have realised,' said Fyn. 'If Dad could have come back, he would have. It should have been obvious.'

'Listen to me,' said Scott, his voice strong with authority but not unkind. 'Don't let your thoughts get the better of you. I used to think it would *never* be possible to travel between worlds again. The risk of tearing the universes apart was always too great but, rightly or wrongly, here we are. Things are changing.'

Fyn felt the annoyance rush through him again. 'But *you're* the one who brought us here.'

'Please,' Marina pleaded. 'I know it feels hopeless, but you must trust things will work out. You're not alone.'

Fyn was so frustrated. He had every right to feel the way he did. Why should some unknown chance be enough? How could anyone expect that to be okay? He looked out of the window before closing his eyes. Then he sighed. He knew this wasn't her fault. It wasn't *anyone's* fault. He was a guest in their home, and they were only trying to help him. He looked back and saw Rosie sitting on Amy's knee. She wasn't laughing any more. Instead, her bottom lip quivered.

'Sorry, Grandad,' he said more calmly. 'I didn't mean it. I just can't bear the thought of never seeing...' He couldn't bring himself to say the words aloud.

'Me too,' said Amy, and Fyn felt for her. At least he had some family on Eromlos.

Grandad Bernie addressed them both. 'As we keep saying, we *are* in this together. I can assure you you're not the only ones who are upset, but we've still got a good amount of time before anyone is going to wonder where we are – let's use it as best we can. In the meantime, I understand your feelings, but we must try and remember our manners.' He raised his eyebrows pointedly.

'It's okay, Bernie,' said Scott. 'None of this is easy. We should focus on finding Daniel and go from there. I'm sure Rogan will have guidance when we see him later.'

Fyn heard quickly paced footsteps from outside and looked to the doorway.

As if on cue, Lance and Lucas ran up the steps and into the room. Both were flushed with excitement.

'Dad! Dad!' they called.

Scott laughed as he welcomed them in. 'What is it? Have you seen Rogan?'

'Yes!' said Lucas.

'We saw him, Dad! Just like you asked!' said Lance.

Scott smiled. 'And what did he say?'

'He wants everyone in the *whole* village to come to the hall at sundown. He said we should introduce ourselves and have—'

'—a party!' Lucas interrupted. He looked up at them expectantly. Then, suddenly shy, he hid behind his older brother.

'Come out, silly,' said Scott as Lucas shuffled awkwardly. 'That's excellent news. Did he say anything else?'

'Yes,' said Lance, taking the lead again. 'He said your friends can stay in the guest house, but then he said they might want to stay at—'

'—at Daniel's!' said Lucas piping up once again and leaping out from behind Lance, his arms outstretched like a pouncing monster.

Everyone laughed, including Rosie, although Lance looked a little put out at having his big finish stolen.

'How does that sound?' Scott asked Fyn and the others.

Fyn looked excitedly to Grandad Bernie and Amy, the idea of seeing his dad's home cheering him up. 'Amazing! I mean, I'd love to if...'

'It sounds great,' said Grandad Bernie with a smile.

'Perfect!' said Scott, and Fyn felt a warm and comforting glow spread through his chest.

'That's settled then,' said Marina as she got up, 'and I'm not trying to rush you out, but Scott can take you there now and fetch supplies on the way. I'll sort some food and we can eat back here soon.'

'Right you are,' said Scott.

'And I really am sorry,' said Fyn again.

'There's nothing to be sorry about,' Marina replied. 'I'm just grateful you're okay, and that I've been able to meet you.'

Fyn smiled. Partly with thanks, and partly due to his excitement.

Scott led him, Amy, and Grandad Bernie outside with Lance and Lucas, and about halfway down the hill they joined a different path, following it to a building twice the size of the others. The sheet covering its entrance was decorated with a symbol in a similar way to the one at Scott's house but, this time, the circle contained two hands next to each other with their palms facing upwards. They were positioned as if to make an offering, or in readiness to receive something.

'This is the stock shack,' said Scott.

It was a single room full of shelving units, each packed with supplies.

Scott picked up some cream-coloured clothes and shook them out to check the sizes. 'These should do the job.' Then he handed them each a sling. 'I'd put your belongings in these. People here aren't used to backpacks ... or trainers,' he added.

After selecting some surprisingly comfy sandals which had strong rubber soles, they collected a few more bits, and Scott led them back up the main path to a house on the left. This time the circle on the sheet contained a bright sun surrounded by small rays. In between the smaller rays, three larger ones reached to the edges of the circle.

'Have you worked out the symbols yet?' Scott asked.

'I'm not sure,' said Fyn. 'The one at the stock shack seemed to say what the room was for.'

'That's right,' he replied, 'although there is more to them. They *do* identify each type of building, but they're also like a family crest. Each family designs their own and you'll see they have a subtle feature to show how many people live there. Mine has five waves to symbolise Marina, the kids, and me. Daniel's has three main sunbeams to symbolise him, your mother, and you. Even though you weren't here in person, you were always part of him, and you still are.' He pointed to the doorway. 'You should go in first.'

Fyn approached the entrance with Grandad Bernie and Amy close behind. Taking an unsteady breath, he pulled the sheet across and stepped inside.

Walking into the home his dad had lived in for the last eight years, he didn't really know what to expect. Any hopes of seeing him casually pottering about quickly passed. The place was empty.

It was pretty much the same layout as Scott and Marina's, but tidier and less personalised. He wondered how much his dad had taken when he left, then realised he had no idea what he might have owned. He didn't really know him at all.

Inside the room there were a few stools, a table, and a bench. Shelves on the walls were mostly bare but for a few bundles of paper, bound together by fraying string. Had his dad been living like this?

Grandad Bernie and Amy followed him in with Scott, Lance, and Lucas behind them. After putting down the supplies, Scott sent the boys home, watching them wave excitedly as they left.

'So, this is your father's place,' he said afterwards. 'There's a bedroom behind the back wall, and a separate toilet too. You'll want to keep the lid down to prevent the smell, but don't worry,' he said as Fyn grimaced. 'Whoever's on duty will empty the buckets under the house twice a day.'

'Nice,' said Amy rather bluntly.

'There are wipes with your supplies,' continued Scott. 'To freshen up properly, the wash shack is down the hill by the river. You'll work it out, but if you need anything let me know. Otherwise, I'll see you when you're ready for lunch.'

As he walked out and down the porch he called back happily, 'I still can't believe you're here!'

Fyn, Amy, and Grandad Bernie stood in the middle of the room.

Looking back at the sheet hanging over the doorway, Fyn imagined a glorious moment where his dad walked in and ran forward to hug him. He stared and waited, but it didn't happen.

'I guess we'd better get a move on,' said Grandad Bernie, picking up their handmade towels. 'We can sort our things later.'

There was an air of excitement among the villagers who smiled and waved at them on their way to the wash shack. Fyn wondered how many already knew who they were.

He was reassured they were heading in the right direction by a pretty girl about his age wearing a bright yellow robe. Her long brown hair was wet, and she also carried a towel. As she walked past in the opposite direction, she smiled at him.

Caught off guard he nearly tripped over his feet and looked back awkwardly to see her laughing.

Grandad Bernie coughed, and Fyn turned his attention back to where he was going.

The wash shack itself was one of the most bizarre things he had ever experienced. Each partition in the shack had a barrel of cold water, some herby paste, and a bowl. The paste tingled as he rubbed it on his skin. Scooping the water with the bowl he shuddered as he poured it over himself, although he soon got used to it – unlike Grandad Bernie who shrieked every time the water touched his skin.

In their new clothes, and after lunch, they settled back at Fyn's dad's house to rest until the evening. Fyn and Grandad Bernie offered Amy the bedroom and chose to share the main room themselves.

Grandad Bernie took an old watch from his bag and wound it up. Then he set an alarm before spreading a blanket on the floor.

'Don't mind me,' he said, closing his eyes after lying down. 'This nap is thoroughly deserved. Plus, a bit of beauty sleep might help my wrinkles.' He looked at them both again with a cheeky glimmer in his eyes. 'It might be an idea for you to rest up too,' he said before rolling over.

Fyn and Amy left him to it. Fyn wandered round to his dad's bedroom and stepped in.

It felt so strange that there was no real sign of his dad – just a basic bed and a few crates of clothing.

He sighed.

'Everything okay?' Amy asked.

He hadn't noticed she was right beside him. 'I guess so,' he murmured.

She passed him and looked around.

'It's just,' he continued. 'I thought I'd learn more about him by being here, but it's almost like there was no him to know.'

'He definitely missed home,' said Amy, pointing behind him.

Fyn turned around and saw that tally charts had been carved all over the wooden wall next to the doorframe. There must have been thousands of engravings.

He followed them to the end where they stopped next to a tiny message.

No matter how many days pass, my family are with me.

He gulped. If only he could show this to his mum. He stared at the words, letting them sink in and provide the reassurance he'd been seeking for so long. 'We've got to find him,' he said. 'Whatever it takes.'

CHAPTER FOURTEEN
Rogan

At the top of Homehill, as the sun began to sink into the treeline of a crimson sky, Fyn, Amy, and Grandad Bernie arrived with Scott and his family to find a crowd of villagers eagerly awaiting them.

A tall muscular man with mousy-brown hair, handed bands of white flowers to the males to wear around their necks. Next to him, a slim woman with short and spiky black hair handed single white flowers to the females.

Amy copied Marina by placing the flower behind her ear.

Fyn looked down at the floral necklace around his neck and smiled, thinking it was actually kind of cool – a bit like the Hawaiian leis he had seen on tv.

A post with a flaming torch stood in the centre of a clearing with a building on either side. One was much larger than the other buildings in the village. The front beams were carved to look like twisting vines, and palm trees swayed at its sides. The other was more like the homes he'd seen, and he guessed it belonged to Rogan.

They congregated with the villagers around the house, and the sheet across the doorway shimmered in the last sunlight of the day. Like the other sheets, it had a circular symbol, but this one was golden, and silver thread linked it to many smaller designs spread across the fabric. His dad's design was one of them.

'Rogan symbolises his family as the entire village,' Scott said to Fyn and the others. 'Daniel's crest is there, and so is mine,' he pointed a bit to the right.

The sheet moved aside, and everyone stopped talking. A man walked out onto the porch. He was old – older than Grandad Bernie. His short hair and beard were grey, and his wrinkled skin carved deep grooves into his face. He was slender and fragile looking – not what Fyn had expected for a leader.

Fyn looked up at Scott. 'Is that...?'

'Yes,' he replied. 'That's Rogan.'

Rogan moved forward and was slightly hunched on his way down the steps. He greeted the villagers like greeting old friends as he walked into the crowd holding and shaking their hands, his eyes wide and alive with happiness. As he gently held up one hand, any new conversations stopped.

'Welcome everyone,' he said, and Fyn was surprised at how strongly his voice carried across the crowd.

'Thank you for coming together at such short notice. We are most fortunate to be joined tonight by some wonderful guests, and it's very important to make them feel welcome. As we say goodbye to the sun for today,' he waved one arm slowly through the air, 'let us now greet the night together.'

It was perfectly timed. The sun disappeared below the horizon and the villagers erupted into applause, celebrating the end of the day.

Together, they moved into the hall. It was lit by candles floating in small bowls of water that rested on pillars around the room. As people settled onto the rows of benches, their shadows dashed across the walls and the atmosphere began to feel thick with anticipation.

Rogan sat at the front to face them, and there were three empty seats beside him.

'They're for you,' said Scott, much to Fyn's dismay.

Trying to ignore the faces staring at him and the others, he sat next to Amy and Grandad Bernie.

Scott and his family sat directly opposite on the first row of benches. Then the room fell silent as Rogan stood.

'Today,' he began, 'I've heard many rumours and I know the village is excited. Some say our honoured guests have come from afar. This is true. Others say they are related to one of our own, and this is also true. Finally, I've even heard they're aliens!' He laughed. 'Well, everyone could be an alien in the right place at the right time, but the simpler truth is our guests are the family and friends of Daniel.'

The villagers soaked in every word, eagerly waiting to discover the next piece of information as Rogan's voice filled the hall.

'They arrived this morning and have travelled from the same region Scott and Daniel came from many years ago.'

Scott smirked at Fyn who remembered not everyone knew about world windows.

'Receiving visitors like this,' Rogan continued, 'would normally be cause for celebration, but I must ask us to hold on a little longer as we discuss recent events.'

Heads nodded in agreement throughout the hall and a voice called from the crowd, 'Is there news on Daniel?'

'Not yet,' Rogan replied calmly, and an uncomfortable muttering broke out among the villagers, '...but progress is being made and please be assured there is no evidence of wrongdoing. However, while there is no severe cause for concern, I would advise you all to include caution in your activities.'

'Why did the guardians visit Homehill last night?' came a different voice. 'What were they looking for?'

A shiver ran through the room. Fyn watched as the villagers shifted nervously in their seats.

Rogan spoke with warmth and confidence. 'We have no reason to fear them despite their actions. They were investigating a disturbance, and I doubt they'll question us about it any more. If they do, you can always direct them to me.' He smiled. 'Please do ask me questions outside if you need to, but for now let us return to introductions.'

He turned to Fyn, Amy, and Grandad Bernie.

'I am Rogan, and I am the so-called "head" of the village, but I'm no more important than anyone else here. If there were no village, I would only be a head of myself so to speak. It's a privilege to meet you.'

He leaned forward and shook hands with each of them in turn. His hands felt warm and wrinkly, like he'd been in a bath for too long.

'If you would be so kind and not in any way intimidated by your humble audience, it would be our honour to hear from you. Be as fancy as you please, but your names and connection to Daniel will suffice if words fail you.'

Expectation filled the room as he sat down, and Fyn felt torn as to whether or not he should stand. It was with relief that he saw Grandad Bernie do it first.

'Good evening,' he said quietly before clearing his throat and speaking louder. 'I am Bernie, and I am Daniel's father. I'm beyond grateful to be here, and more thankful to you all than I can express for giving him a home for so long.' He looked at them for a moment. 'I hope we find him soon, and I thank you for your hospitality while we stay.' Then he gave a polite little nod before settling back in his seat.

Fyn looked at Amy, but she didn't move at all, so he decided to stand next.

'Hi,' he said, feeling nervous and resisting the urge to sit right back down. 'My name is Fyn, and Daniel is my dad.'

Light muttering started again but stopped when he continued to speak.

'It's been so long since I've seen him; I wasn't sure if I ever would again...' He watched everyone staring at him in the candlelight and felt uneasy for a moment. If they didn't all know where his dad was from, maybe they didn't all understand why he had travelled to Homehill and left his family. 'I know he misses us too,' he said by way of explanation, thinking of the carvings on his dad's bedroom wall, 'and I can't wait to see him again.'

Scott and Marina grinned at him encouragingly.

'Thanks,' said Fyn as he sat down.

Amy stood next. She held her hands tight behind her back.

'Umm... Hi everyone,' she mumbled, much to Fyn's surprise. 'I'm Amy, and well ... I'm not related to Daniel or Scott, but Daniel and my parents were friends, and Fyn and I have been besties forever.'

She paused and looked down at her feet.

Fyn wondered if she had lost her train of thought, but she looked back up and continued.

'I'll do anything I can to support his family because they're family to me. They mean the world to me actually. So, umm... Thank you, and umm... Yeah, thanks.'

She sat back down with her arms firmly at her sides and looked anywhere but at the crowd.

Rogan stood once more. 'Our guests will be staying at Daniel's, at least for tonight. So, with that in mind, let us make them feel welcome!' He threw his arms out wide, and the villagers cheered as they began to leave the hall.

Rogan turned to Fyn and the others. 'If you could hold on for a while longer... There is more you need to know.'

CHAPTER FIFTEEN

The Plan

Fyn watched as Marina left the hall with Lance, Lucas, and Rosie. Scott remained, as did a man and woman in the second row with – he did a double take – the girl from their walk to the wash shack earlier that afternoon. She was sitting next to a boy around the same age. Only two others remained: the slim woman with short, spiky hair and the tall muscular man who had given them their decorative flowers. The latter pulled the sheet across the doorway after the last of the villagers left. Then he joined the others at the front.

'It is time, Dimitry,' said Rogan.

Fyn was not the only one who jumped as a man with black hair tied back in a ponytail appeared out of nowhere, phasing into appearance in the corner closest to them.

'Sheesh!' shouted Scott.

The spiky-haired woman laughed. 'How long have you been there?'

'The whole time,' said the man, as if he had done nothing more interesting than pull on a pair of socks.

'Dimitry,' explained Rogan, 'is not from this village. He is a dealer of information – a spy if you will – and can be a hard man to track. He and his partner Florentina have been working to try and find Daniel, but three days ago Florentina was captured by agents.' His voice had lost the warmth from minutes ago and was now gravely serious.

'I visited Daniel a few weeks before he disappeared,' he continued, 'and found him deeply troubled. He wouldn't tell me why. Instead, he sought my discretion, assuring me he would tell me more if his suspicions were confirmed. That was the last time I saw him.'

Fyn didn't understand. 'No one knows why he left?'

'Or what was bothering him?' Grandad Bernie asked. 'Do you think his concerns are why he went missing?'

'I suspect that is the case,' replied Rogan. He grimaced, making his wrinkly face crinkle even more. When he spoke next he sounded calculated, like every word was the result of considerable thought.

'The agents guard powerful secrets in their citadel, south of here in the City of the Sea, but it is my belief that they do not know how to fully access them. If they've discovered

Daniel's scientific nature, he may look to them like the key to a hidden treasure. We must stop them from using him that way. I am a spiritual man, and I don't say this lightly – I sense we are closer to disaster now than we have ever been.'

The words spread over them like a harsh reality, the air itself feeling heavier somehow.

'Even if they know he's a scientist,' said Fyn, 'why would that make them think he could help with secrets like that? Does it have something to do with the work he's been doing here?'

'Yes,' replied Rogan. 'I've long suspected the desires of the agents and their masters, so I have been working with Scott and Daniel to seek a safe way to travel between worlds – in case we should need to stand against them. With the use of technology so limited for us, it has been slow progress and mostly theory. The agents don't have that problem so could work far more freely with Scott and Daniel than I, but the further they take the work, the greater the risk of consequences. We have no idea how fragile the lining between universes may be or the amount of disruption it would take for a new catastrophe to strike. If they have Daniel and force his work, it could be the tipping point that starts the end of everything.'

Fyn felt the sting from the reminder that, even if they found his dad, it wasn't safe yet for them to travel home.

'What about the device that brought us here?' Amy asked. 'That seems to work. Can we not use it again?'

'The only times we've used it for travelling,' replied Rogan, 'are in cases of life and death and even then it was at great risk. We should restrict use of it to communications, and only where there is no alternative. The agents are ever watching.'

Scott shuffled slightly at Rogan's words, but Fyn no longer blamed him for bringing them to Eromlos. He had to believe there was a way home. At least being here brought him closer to his dad.

'And what happens if the agents get hold of it?' Amy continued.

'We must never let them know it exists but, if they ever found out and took it, I'd hope they'd use it sparingly. That said, it is possible they may try and force someone like Daniel to help them understand it.'

'Rogan,' said the woman with short, spiky hair. 'Do you believe that Daniel left or that he was taken?'

He looked lost in thought for a moment. 'I suspect he left of his own accord, perhaps to avoid endangering others. Still, I believe we know enough to form a plan.' He gestured to the short-haired woman. 'This is Mya. She is highly skilled in many areas including combat, hunting, and cooking a rather tasty berry waffle.'

Mya smiled but her arms remained tightly folded.

'Here we have Art, who is as gentle-minded as he is strong and courageous.'

The muscular man gave a brief wave.

'Last from the village, we have Nico and Eva, and their twins Theo and Kallista.'

'Please, call me Kali,' said the girl.

'My apologies,' Rogan replied. 'Nico and Eva take the lead on training and supplies. Theo and Kali are highly skilled in those areas but can be somewhat ... shall we say ... over-adventurous?'

Theo and Kali smirked mischievously at each other.

'Finally, and as I'm sure has been shocked into your memory,' said Rogan, 'this is Dimitry.'

The man who had appeared from nowhere gave a sharp nod.

'Dimitry arrived after you today,' Rogan said to Scott, 'and I propose a party sets out to rescue Florentina first thing in the morning. If willing, I'd like all of you here from the village to be part of the group. Our hope is Florentina may have discovered news on Daniel, so upon finding her I imagine the group may split, with some returning home to provide an update, and others continuing on as proves necessary.'

'Count me in,' said Mya.

'And us,' said Nico after briefly consulting with Eva and the twins.

'I'll happily help,' said Art, and Fyn felt grateful and somewhat humbled that all these strangers were willing to put themselves at risk for his dad.

'Thank you,' said Rogan. 'I confess I expected as much. Now, please forgive my saying so, but I believe it may be better Bernie, Fyn, and Amy, for you to stay here until we know more.'

Fyn opened his mouth to challenge, but Rogan cut in.

'It will be a dangerous mission, and none of you really understand *this* world. Yes, everyone in this room knows where you're from,' he added calmly, 'although the rest of the village does not.'

Fyn looked Rogan in the eyes. 'Please, I can't just stay here and wait. I'll do whatever I can to help, but I need to go. It's my dad.'

'We can watch out for him,' Scott said to Rogan. 'If you can do what we ask,' he added to Fyn.

Fyn nodded vigorously. 'I can!'

'Not without me!' said Amy.

Fyn saw Kali look at her curiously.

'...and what about *me?*' asked Grandad Bernie. 'You can't expect me to let you two go off gallivanting around some other world on your own, with or without a group! What kind of grandfather would I be?'

'The best kind!' said Fyn.

'Be that as it may...'

'Come with us,' urged Amy. 'You don't have to stay behind'.

'Actually,' said Scott, 'it's not that I wouldn't want you along, Bernie, but it might be good for someone to stay in case Daniel returns.'

Grandad Bernie raised an eyebrow. 'Very tactful, but I think Rogan has a point. We don't know this place and our inexperience could endanger not only others but ourselves too.'

Fyn felt his insides shift. He didn't like where this was going.

Grandad Bernie's face was taut as he spoke to Fyn and Amy. 'I know how much this means to you because I feel it too, and I appreciate you'd look out for them,' he added to Scott, 'but I'm afraid the answer is no.'

'But, Grandad!' Fyn protested.

'No,' Grandad Bernie repeated. 'Risking you and risking the others is too much risk in my book. I'm sorry, but you're my responsibility.'

'But—' Amy started.

'It's no use tag-teaming me,' said Grandad Bernie. 'I've made my decision.'

Fyn huffed and looked at the villagers. Apart from Theo and Kali, they all avoided eye contact.

Theo rolled his eyes as if to say "awkward", making Fyn flush red with embarrassment.

'I understand,' said Scott. 'Not to worry. We'll get news back to you all as soon as we can.'

'That settles it,' said Rogan, as Fyn furiously fought the urge to sulk in front of strangers. 'Those of you going will set out tomorrow morning. For the rest of the evening let us forget our concerns. Dine, dance, and be merry!'

'Not me,' said Dimitry. 'I'll meet the rescue party in the morning.' Then, without another word, he phased out of sight.

'A man of many talents!' said Rogan, making his way to the exit.

As they left the village hall to join the others, Fyn felt so frustrated. Why couldn't he and Amy be trusted? He was sure there had to be a way they could help, and he had until morning to figure it out.

CHAPTER SIXTEEN

Fire Demon

As bitter as Fyn felt for not being allowed to join the rescue party, he couldn't help but enjoy the celebrations.

The villagers danced and they sang. They played games and told stories. They prepared a huge feast of food with fresh flame-grilled fish, poultry, and all kinds of strange roasted vegetables. There was nothing not to like – apart from the mussels. Their thick, slimy texture reminded him of a nasty cold from a few years back…

Throughout the night, everyone wanted to introduce themselves to him, Amy, and Grandad Bernie. It was very nice, but at the same time it made it hard for Fyn to speak to Amy alone. As the night progressed, he began to feel desperate. They had to find a way to join the others on their rescue mission. If only he could be there to help save

Florentina, it would be like he was also helping his dad somehow.

'We need more food!' one of the villagers shouted. 'Who's going to the stock shack?'

Fyn seized the opportunity. 'We can! What would you like?'

'Surprise us!' the villager called back.

Fyn smiled and grabbed Amy by the arm. 'Come on!'

Grandad Bernie watched them closely. 'Don't be long.'

'We won't,' Fyn replied, already on his way down the hill.

Listening to the celebrations continue behind them, they ventured towards the shack. Amy nudged him and pointed towards Scott and Marina's house as they passed it. Scott and Marina were outside.

Fyn went to wave but thought better of it as he heard their raised voices.

'I know how important it is,' Marina said to Scott. 'I really do, but I can't help how I feel. You've only just got back. It's not safe out there.'

'I promise I'll take care,' Scott assured her. 'I don't want to leave any of you behind, but this is for the greater good.' He held her shoulders.

She embraced him, but Fyn could have sworn she was crying as she went quiet.

Feeling sad for Marina and as though they shouldn't have witnessed the conversation, he looked away. The last thing he wanted was to be caught eavesdropping. Especially in such a sensitive moment.

He didn't feel any better when they reached the stock shack, but he knew this was their chance to talk.

Pulling the sheet aside he stepped in. It was so dark he could hardly see a thing.

Amy rubbed her hand absent-mindedly on the wall, seeking a light switch which wasn't there. 'I don't think we thought this through,' she said. 'I'll keep the sheet held aside. Maybe that will help'.

'Thanks,' he replied, beginning to scan the shelves in the dark and trying to remember the layout from earlier. 'It's so weird, isn't it? I mean, no technology unless you're the baddie. It's so unfair for everyone else.'

'I know,' said Amy, keeping watch without really needing to. 'The people here must be really strong. I hope we can help them somehow.'

'Me too,' he replied, venturing further in.

'What's your thinking for tomorrow? We can't just up and leave in the morning. They'll never let us.'

'I wouldn't do that to Grandad Bernie,' said Fyn. 'I was just hoping there would be something we could do to convince him we'd be alright.'

'I doubt it,' said Amy.

Something sounded briefly from behind the shelves at the back of the room.

'What was that?' Amy asked.

Not wanting to reply in case whatever it was could hear him, he looked back and shrugged. Then he continued walking quietly alongside the shelving, wondering what kind of rats they might have in Eromlos ... and how big they might be.

His heart skipped a beat as the sound resumed, like something was scratching against or digging into a crate. Whatever it was, it either didn't care that he was there, or it hadn't heard him.

That didn't last. Fyn yelped in shock as he caught his foot on something in the dark.

The sound stopped immediately, and whatever had made the noise burst out from behind the shelves, rushing past him.

Amy leapt aside as it shot out the door.

'What was it?' Fyn asked.

'I don't know,' she replied. 'I looked away when it ran at me!'

He joined her at the entrance and scanned the hill in the moonlight, but there was no sign of it. 'Come on. Let's grab some food and get out of here.'

Returning to the shelves he picked up a bunch of yellow sleeves with some berries, and as they walked back up to the celebrations, Scott and Marina were nowhere to be seen. Fyn wondered if they'd returned to the party or gone to bed.

He was about to discuss the conversation they'd overheard when a piercing scream came from the top of the hill.

The happy sounds and music cut out.

Dropping the fruit, Fyn started to run. 'What *now?*' he called on the way, keen to return to the safety of the crowd and find out what was happening.

Grandad Bernie rushed over to them as they reached the top of Homehill. 'Thank goodness you're back.'

'What's going on?' Fyn asked.

'I'm not sure,' he replied. 'Someone screamed. There's talk of a demon.'

Fyn shifted nervously. *Could it be the creature from the stock shack?*

He looked to Amy, but she was distracted by the villagers who were huddled together, watching a smaller group scout out the back of Rogan's house.

'It can't have been a demon though,' Grandad Bernie backtracked. 'I'm sure there's nothing to worry about.'

'There!' shouted a villager.

'What is it?' another called.

'A fire demon!' the first replied.

Fyn and Amy huddled closer to Grandad Bernie.

'Stick together,' he said. 'We'll be fine.'

'There it goes!' someone shouted, and the people around Rogan's house separated, allowing something small to run straight towards Fyn, Amy, and Grandad Bernie.

Several people shouted, but Grandad Bernie gasped, 'I don't believe it!'

Fyn was ready to jump out of the way when he recognised the familiar orange fuzzball. He felt a rush of relief and excitement as Henry Flame ran up to them and ducked behind their legs.

'It's okay,' Grandad Bernie called to the villagers. 'There's no need to panic!'

The people of Homehill stared at them warily.

'It's bright like fire!' one of the men called. 'It tried to attack one of the long necks.'

'The what?' Fyn asked.

Scott ran over to their side. 'They're like chickens but with necks so long they can reach the grain at the top of tall grass.' He looked to the villagers. 'There's nothing to worry about. The creature you see, it's not a demon. It's called a fox.'

The villagers muttered uncertainly.

'I've never seen anything like it,' one of them called.

Fyn knelt down and let a cowering Henry Flame sniff his hand. 'It's okay,' he whispered calmly. 'We'll protect you.'

'He's our friend,' said Amy. 'He must have followed us here. We call him Henry Flame.'

The muttering continued.

'Flame like fire,' one said. 'It *is* a fire demon!'

'It won't hurt you,' said Scott. 'Trust me.'

'Calm down, everyone! Calm down,' Rogan's voice rang out through the crowd.

He walked to the front of the villagers and looked from Fyn and the others to Henry Flame. 'We must have faith in our guests – and in Scott. It's likely the creature is more scared of us than us of it. It might simply be hungry.'

'But the long necks?' one of the villagers challenged.

'We're used to keeping them safe from far worse than the likes of this creature,' Rogan replied calmly.

Before Fyn could wonder what he meant, a humming sound began to fill the sky. His eyes followed it to the distance where he saw bright blue streaks soaring towards them.

Villagers began to cry out in alarm. 'The guardians! The guardians are coming!'

CHAPTER SEVENTEEN

The Raid

'Nobody panic,' Rogan called out to the villagers, but Fyn wasn't convinced his words were working this time.

The crowd looked nervous. He could see it in their darting eyes, and the way they fidgeted like they'd rather be anywhere else.

He watched as the lights from four soarers sped closer to the top of Homehill.

Amy tried to comfort Henry Flame, but he ducked down low to the ground and ran into the shadows.

'He'll come back,' said Grandad Bernie, holding Fyn and Amy before they could follow. 'He knows where we are now.'

Rogan came over and spoke to Scott. 'We mustn't let the agents find them here.'

Scott nodded then turned to Fyn and the others. 'Come with me.'

He led them into the crowd and towards the other side of the hill.

Fyn heard Rogan calling out to the villagers, 'Everybody try to stay calm. Whatever you do, don't tell them of our guests – only that we're celebrating life. Direct them to me if needed!'

'Why are we panicking?' Amy asked as they continued to pass among the villagers. 'I mean, how will the agents know about us?'

'They might not,' Scott replied, 'but we can't take that chance if they ask questions.'

'Plus,' said Grandad Bernie, 'It might be rather obvious.' He looked around.

Nearly everyone they passed was watching them as they went.

One of the soarers reached the top of Homehill and hovered above the crowd. The other three rotated around it, then all four shone beams of white light on everyone, halting them on the spot.

Fyn raised a hand above his eyes and squinted.

'Stay where you are,' a loud voice announced from a speaker on the central soarer.

'We should do as they say,' Scott warned. 'We'll stand out even more if we don't.'

Fyn gulped.

The three rotating soarers stopped in mid-air before lowering cords. Agents in dark grey uniforms slid down them to the edges of the crowd.

With fewer eyes watching from the sky, Scott dared to move them a little more.

'Stay where you are,' the voice repeated from the soarer above, 'and no harm will come to you.'

'Just move very slowly,' said Scott. 'We can't stay here.'

It turned out that *slowly* was the only way they could go. As the agents on the outskirts of the crowd began to question the villagers, the inner crowd became more compacted, and it was harder to move.

Feeling trapped and helpless, Fyn began taking deeper breaths.

'It's okay,' said Grandad Bernie. 'We'll be out soon.'

'I can help,' came a voice from beside them. Then, in the same way that he had back in the village hall, the man named Dimitry phased into appearance.

The villagers around them didn't seem to notice, but Fyn was so startled it distracted him from fretting, even as more people bumped into them.

'You're going to have to stop doing that,' Amy said to Dimitry, her hand on her chest. 'You'll give someone a heart attack!'

Fyn instinctively checked on Grandad Bernie.

'Don't worry about me, short stuff,' he said. 'I may be old but I'm still healthy.'

Dimitry glanced at Amy but ignored her comment. 'I can't help you all, but I can hide two of you – at least for long enough to get out of here.'

'Hide the children, please,' said Scott.

Fyn was about to protest the use of the word "children", but Dimitry took a hold of his and Amy's shoulders.

His perspective completely changed.

He could see everything happening around him, but it seemed slower, and the sounds were audible but muffled. He looked at Amy, and then up to Dimitry who nodded knowingly.

'They're definitely still here?' Grandad Bernie asked, as though on the other side of an invisible barrier. His eyes were wide.

'Yes,' said Scott, 'although I'm not sure how it works. Stay slow but come with me.'

They all edged nearer to the outskirts of the crowd who were no longer looking at Fyn, Amy, or Dimitry.

The agents worked their way through villagers nearby, asking them for signs of disturbances, assuring them it was safe to speak up.

Scott waited for the right moment. 'Quickly,' he said, leading them out of the crowd and towards the village hall when the agents faced the other way. He got there first and ducked around the side, followed closely by Grandad Bernie.

A number of villagers watched, and an agent followed their gaze.

'Hurry,' Fyn hissed quietly, as he, Amy, and Dimitry joined Scott and Grandad Bernie. 'I think someone saw you.'

'Don't speak,' said Dimitry, but it was too late.

Somehow Fyn's voice had broken their illusion. He, Amy, and Dimitry became visible again.

'Come on!' said Scott, pulling them into the cover of the trees.

'We won't get far like this,' whispered Dimitry. 'There are too many of us to hide.'

Fyn looked around anxiously. 'What can we do?'

Grandad Bernie turned to Scott. 'You'll look after them?'

Scott's expression shifted from serious to concerned as he realised what Grandad Bernie was asking of him. 'I'll keep them as safe as I would my own children.'

'Grandad...' said Fyn. 'No...'

'You can't...' said Amy.

'Take them...' said Grandad Bernie, ignoring them both.

'Grandad!' Fyn repeated, almost forgetting to be quiet. 'We can't leave you!'

'There's no time,' said Grandad Bernie as he stepped out from the trees. 'If I stay I'll slow you down. I'll distract them instead. Make your father as proud as you've made me.' He looked to Dimitry and nodded.

'I'll look after them,' said Scott.

Dimitry re-established the illusion hiding Fyn and Amy as the agent rounded the back of the village hall and spotted Grandad Bernie.

Scott shifted to hide, but a branch snapped beneath his feet.

The agent started to look in their direction.

Grandad Bernie cleared his throat and pulled the agent's attention. Then, and to the surprise of everyone, he began to sing. '*I foollooowed my heart because I kneeeew, it was the very best way to get back to yooou!*' He pretended to hiccup, held a finger to his lips as if to shush the agent, and turned in a circle on the spot to bow dramatically.

Fyn felt his heart drop as the agent pointed some kind of baton from his arm and steered Grandad Bernie towards the crowd.

Dimitry held Fyn still, and it was only as Grandad Bernie and the agent were out of sight that Fyn reluctantly allowed himself to be led into the jungle.

CHAPTER EIGHTEEN

A Spy's Tale

Within a few minutes the tree cover was so thick there was no sign of Homehill at all – only glimpses of the light from the soarers hovering above the village they'd left behind.

Dimitry let go of Fyn and Amy, phasing them all back into view.

Scott, who had been looking back for a sign of them, stopped. 'Thank goodness you're still with me. I know this is off plan. No supplies. Mostly no rescue party.'

'We could go back...' said Fyn, '...wait and see what happens. Get Grandad—'

'—It's too risky,' Scott interrupted. 'Your grandad will be fine. We have to keep going and hope the right people track us when they can.'

Fyn wanted to argue but Amy held his arm and shook her head. 'I know,' she whispered. 'I do, but Grandad Bernie saved us. He knew what he was doing. We have to trust him. What if we got caught and ruined everything?'

He frowned. He knew Grandad Bernie was capable but that didn't make it easier to leave him.

'At least we're on the mission now,' she continued. 'It's sort of what we...'

He guessed why she trailed off. It felt like she was about to say, "what we wanted", but he never wanted it to be like this. Two nights in and two run-ins with the agents. What chance did they have without Grandad Bernie?

'Dimitry,' said Scott, 'you know the mission. We're in your hands.'

His attention brought back to the spy, Fyn marvelled at the way he had hidden them and how things had changed when they were concealed. 'How did you...? How do you...?' He couldn't find the words. 'I've never seen anything like it before.'

'It's part of the ways of my people,' Dimitry replied, 'and those ways are sworn to secrecy.'

'You mean there are *more* things you can do?' Amy asked in awe.

Dimitry smirked before facing the darkness and leading them ahead.

The next morning, after trekking into the early hours, Fyn woke to the sound of the bugs, birds, and creatures of the jungle. Something brushed against his hand. Nervous to look, he glanced down and his chest swelled with happiness as he saw Henry Flame looking up at him.

'I'm so glad you're okay!' he whispered in relief. He held his hand flat beneath the young fox's nose and felt it tickle him as the orange fuzzball had a good sniff. When he didn't run away, Fyn gave him a gentle rub behind the ears. It was all very well following Grandad Bernie's advice and trying to keep him separate from people back on Earth, but things were different now.

He looked over and saw Amy sleeping against a tree. Scott and Dimitry were awake and talking quietly a little way off.

'Let's stick together, shall we?' he said softly to Henry Flame. 'I don't think the people here are used to foxes.'

Henry Flame licked his hand in response.

When Amy woke she was equally excited at his return, and they found a vine they could loosely use as a lead. At first he resisted, preferring to pull it with his teeth, but after a few attempts he accepted it without too much difficulty.

It wasn't long before they were on their way again and following Dimitry. They travelled, mostly in silence, for the whole morning, with Henry Flame frequently stopping to sniff. Fyn wanted to talk about events from the night before, but it didn't feel appropriate. Scott seemed especially distracted, and Fyn couldn't help but feel a little guilty at the thought of how sad Marina had been and the way Scott had left his family behind.

Dimitry held up his arm to halt them next to a small stream that flowed under the shelter of an especially large tree. 'This is as good a spot as we will find. There's fruit nearby and the water is fresh – as your little friend already knows.'

Fyn looked down to see Henry Flame drinking happily at the edge of the stream.

'We have made good time,' Dimitry continued. 'Rest a moment and I'll tell of Florentina's capture.'

Fyn's attention was caught.

They picked some purple pods and sat beside the stream, a captive audience for Dimitry who looked each of them in the eyes before he spoke.

'Florentina and I decided the best way to discover if agents have captured Daniel would be to investigate the Southern Tower.'

'You're kidding?' Scott asked, seeming both surprised and impressed.

'Dangerous, yes,' Dimitry flitted his hand dismissively, 'but necessary. Stealth is the business of people like me and, doing what we do, situations like that are unavoidable.'

'What's the Southern Tower?' asked Amy, 'I mean, apart from what it sounds like.'

'An agent base,' Scott replied. 'One of many, but this one is in the middle of the jungle. Travelling agents use it to rest and resupply.'

'We decided to approach in the early evening,' Dimitry continued, 'because people are usually ready to relax then and may be less alert. The tower is seven floors high, and the first five are covered by the treetops. We settled on a branch close to a window on the fourth floor and observed until nightfall. Once dark, we tested our luck and went in.'

Fyn continued to chew the purple pods and discard their tough exteriors while listening. No longer grossed out by them, he quite enjoyed the juicy sweetness as they burst in his mouth.

'Then we heard the humming,' said Dimitry. 'The trees rustled and glowed blue. Several soarers descended from the sky, flying past the window we'd just entered. When they landed, agents came into the tower.'

'Did you try to leave?' asked Amy.

'No,' Dimitry replied, 'but we were extra mindful of the threat. We concentrated on blending our energy into our surroundings – you've seen how it helps us hide – then we split up. I took the floor above, and Florentina the one below.'

'Is that when things went wrong?' asked Fyn.

Dimitry squinted at him as though unsure whether to be offended by the question.

Fyn looked away but, rather than answer, Dimitry simply continued.

'There was nothing of interest upstairs, so I went back to the fourth floor. That's when Florentina called out. It was something we'd practiced in advance - like a war cry so it could sound like she was angry rather than give me away like a call for help might.'

'It must have been painful to hear,' said Scott.

Dimitry looked at the ground. 'Knowing she was in danger was piercing to my soul. Every part of me wanted to help her.' He looked back up. 'I sped down the stairs in time to see her captured, under a net, and surrounded by agents. Her eyes warned me away and I blended my appearance into the closest wall. It nearly burst my heart to leave her, but it's one thing to conceal yourself, and another to do so from so many when controlling your emotions. I couldn't chance us both being captured. I knew I needed to leave and replan.'

Fyn looked at Dimitry with interest. He'd never met anyone like him and wondered what Florentina would be like. Then he asked himself, *Would I have been able to resist*

148

rushing in to save the people I love? He could only hope to be strong enough to face the challenges ahead.

CHAPTER NINETEEN

Reunion

Fyn continued to feel guilty about Scott as they travelled towards the Southern Tower. He knew all too well how it felt to miss family and, as he watched him stare into the distance and rarely speak, he worried how Scott felt about leaving his own.

On their third evening since leaving Homehill, they reached some ruins in the jungle. The ancient walls were crumbling, broken apart by enormous roots from trees above which wound down and around the rubble before spreading across the moss-covered floor.

As Amy explored with Henry Flame, Fyn walked around the area and found an entrance to a long-abandoned room. Similar to the towering stones by the clifftop the night they'd arrived on Eromlos, the walls here were also covered with strange markings. *At night it could be creepy*, he thought. For now though, with the birds still chirping and cheering, it wasn't too bad. Traces of sunlight reached inside, and his shadow stretched out across the broken branches and old leaves that had come to rest over time.

'From an age before the agents took control,' said Scott behind him, 'and a good place to stop for the night.'

Later, and after clearing out the room, they sat to eat a selection of fruit. Scott settled between Fyn and Amy who were next to a resting Henry Flame and opposite Dimitry. 'It's a different way of life here isn't it?' Scott suggested.

'Definitely,' said Fyn, feeling slightly uncomfortable at the idea of Scott's family coming up in conversation. He leaned over to stroke Henry Flame.

'The technology thing doesn't sit well with everyone,' Scott admitted, 'but mostly it's the accepted way of things. It's been this way for so many years now. If I'm honest, I quite like it – I mean, the simpler living part; not the oppression.'

'Of course,' said Fyn.

'I get that,' said Amy. 'I love the way everything seems so natural, and I don't know if it's because we're so distracted, but I'm not even really missing the internet.'

'*Ah*, the internet,' said Fyn fondly, thinking back to his adventures in online gaming.

Dimitry's expression was blank.

Fyn wondered if he even knew what they were talking about.

'I do miss hot food though,' Amy continued. 'I mean, what I'd give right now for some of my mum's rice and peas.'

'Now *there's* a memory,' said Scott, 'and that's saying something after so long. It's not the lack of technology stopping us from cooking though. It's just that we can't light a fire in case the smoke gives us away.'

'I know,' said Amy, 'but I can dream.' She looked up and into some imaginary distance.

Scott looked back to Fyn. 'Your father ... I can't describe how amazed he would be.'

Fyn stopped eating mid-mouthful and waited for him to continue.

'I mean, forget that he's a scientist at heart and his son travelling between worlds would be enough for him to smile every day for the rest of his life. Look at what you're doing. You're on a rescue mission in another universe. It's courageous. It's inspired. It's brilliant. The same for you, Amy. I don't know if you'll tell your parents about this someday, but you can be sure they'd also be so proud.'

'Thanks,' she said with a smile.

Fyn was touched too. 'Yes, thank you,' he replied after swallowing, 'but, I can't imagine doing anything else.'

'Me neither,' said Amy.

'That's what makes it so special,' said Scott. 'I'll be proud if any of my kids grow up with the spirit you've shown.'

There it was. Fyn had the familiar stab of guilt in his chest at the mention of Scott's family.

Henry Flame sat up alert, his ears flickering back and forth.

'He is clever,' said Dimitry.

'What is it?' asked Scott.

'I'm not sure yet,' Dimitry replied. 'I only picked up on something a moment before the fire demon did.'

'He's *not* a fire demon,' said Fyn.

Dimitry just winked at him. 'Stay here. Stay quiet.' Then he left the room, phasing out of visibility on the way.

Henry Flame went out after him.

'Come back,' Fyn called as quietly as he could, but he was already gone.

'He'll be fine,' said Scott. 'He seems to like doing things his way.'

'Are we talking about Henry Flame or Dimitry?' Amy asked.

'Both,' said Scott with a cheeky grin.

They waited in silence, peering out between a gap in the rocky wall, but they saw nothing until Henry Flame returned and Dimitry phased into view next to him.

'Do you *ever* get tired of doing that?' Amy asked after jumping once again.

'Never,' said Dimitry, the hint of a smile curving his lips. 'Although, it seems this one can sense me even when I'm hidden,' he indicated Henry Flame.

Fyn was curious, but more so about what they'd heard.

'Wait for it,' said Dimitry. 'They'll be here soon.'

Fyn returned to watching through the gap in the wall until he saw four of the villagers he recognised from Homehill: Art – the large muscular man, Mya – the slim lady with spiky hair, and the twins, Theo and Kali.

Scott sprang up to greet them.

Fyn and Amy followed, but Fyn couldn't help looking past the arrivals in the hope of seeing Grandad Bernie.

'It's just us,' said Mya, 'but your grandad is safe.'

Fyn closed his eyes as a weight lifted from his shoulders.

'This way,' said Scott, leading them into the room and offering them food.

'We brought some supplies,' said Art, reaching to take the sling from his back. He pulled out some bundles of fabric and handed them to Fyn, Amy, Scott, and Dimitry.

'Our stuff!' said Fyn, realising it was his sling with the things that he'd previously kept in his backpack. 'That's great! Thanks!'

'Your grandad thought you'd like them,' said Art with a smile.

'He was right,' said Amy, pulling out a bag of dried apricots which she offered around.

Dimitry opened the sling he'd been given.

'We couldn't leave you out,' said Mya.

'Most kind,' he replied.

Mya took some coconuts from her own sling and passed a couple to Kali. The two of them were carrying bows and arrows.

Using arrow heads, they pierced the eyes at the end of the coconuts to create little drink holes before handing them out.

Henry Flame sniffed around them all.

'He's not so scary now,' said Theo.

'You were scared of him before?' asked Kali.

'No!' he replied, screwing up his face.

'What happened after we left?' asked Scott. 'How is everyone?'

'They're fine,' said Mya. 'All safe. Your family send their love.'

Scott breathed a sigh of relief, and a little bit of Fyn's guilt eased away.

'Your grandad was impressive,' Kali said to Fyn. 'He just acted confused, like he'd had too much cane juice. The agents pretty much ignored him after that.'

Fyn smiled.

'What did they want?' Scott asked.

'They said they were following up on the night before,' said Mya.

'When you arrived,' Theo said to Fyn and Amy.

'I think they must have seen the celebration and decided to round us up,' said Mya, ignoring him. 'No one let anything slip.'

'Thankfully, you got away,' said Art.

'So, what's the plan?' asked Theo. 'Tell me it's something good after we spent so long tracking you?'

'Your timing's ideal,' said Dimitry. 'We'll be up early and arrive at the Southern Tower before sunrise.'

'Seriously?' asked Kali. 'The Southern Tower? That's amazing!'

She rolled her eyes at their bewildered expressions. 'I can't help it if I find it a little exciting!'

'You're with us to report back to Homehill when we know more,' said Mya. 'That's the only reason your parents allowed you to join us. You'll be playing it safe, as will Fyn and Amy I assume?' She looked at Scott.

'For sure,' he replied.

'Good,' she said, before Fyn or Amy could say anything. 'Now let's discuss the details. Tomorrow is creeping closer.'

CHAPTER TWENTY

The Southern Tower

Fyn felt a hand on his arm and opened his eyes. In the shelter of the ruins it was initially too dark to see much of anything.

'We're getting ready,' said Amy, beside him. 'Do you want to share a yellow sleeve?'

He thought of the banana-like fruits.

'No, thanks,' he replied groggily. 'I mean, yes, please, but not yet. What time is it?'

'No idea. I think it's still the middle of the night. It's either too late or too early.'

It occurred to him what they were about to do. For a moment he felt the urge to be anywhere else – until he remembered why they were doing it and how important it was. He heard others up and moving around.

'They're sorting their supplies,' Amy said. 'I don't think they were worried about us sleeping a bit longer. I doubt we'll be doing as much as them anyway.' It wasn't exactly a complaint, but she didn't sound pleased.

They were soon trudging through the undergrowth, Fyn holding Henry Flame's vine to keep them together in the moonlight.

He wondered how they even knew where they were going, but after a long while of slow walking, Dimitry stopped them.

'The clearing around the tower is fifty paces ahead. Mya, are you ready?'

'Yes,' she replied from somewhere to the right of Fyn.

'Good,' said Dimitry. 'We'll move closer. I'll climb up to see what I can, and when I return, you can prepare the diversion. With the agents out of the way, we'll disable any soarers we find before moving in. Expect resistance. If Florentina is still in there, she'll be guarded. Theo and Kallista, you'll be—'

'—waiting out of sight, ready to protect Amy and Fyn if anything comes their way,' said Theo in a very bored voice.

'We don't need protecting,' Amy challenged Theo.

'And it's *Kali*, not Kallista,' Kali remarked.

'This isn't the time!' said Scott. 'We're here to get a job done and lives depend on it. Are you in or not?'

Everyone agreed they were in.

'Good,' said Scott. 'Now let's go. Follow Dimitry.'

'He's certainly got the parenting thing down,' Amy muttered as they walked to the edge of the clearing.

'May our souls survive if our bodies fry,' Fyn heard Mya whisper to herself.

The Southern Tower stood out against the dark blue of the night sky, and light streamed across the grass from its entrance. A few windows were lit on various floors and the sound of men and women laughing came through one of them from somewhere above.

Dimitry vanished up a tree and everyone waited in silence until he returned.

'Four agents in the lit room on the second floor,' he said as he dropped to the ground. 'One in a room on the fifth. I can't tell more than that, and I didn't see Florentina.'

'My turn now,' said Mya, leaving to make her way around the clearing.

'Kali. Theo. Take Fyn and Amy further back,' said Scott. 'Stay clear. All being well, we'll find you soon.'

'Wait,' said Fyn. 'What if it isn't all well?'

'We'll know soon enough,' he replied. 'Stay safe.'

Not feeling comforted at all, Fyn walked further back into the jungle with Amy, Theo, Kali, and Henry Flame.

Theo stopped them sooner than Fyn expected. 'Listen. I know we need to look out for you—'

'—You don't...' Amy interrupted.

'But,' Theo cut back across her, 'we don't need to be far from the others to do that. Let's stay where we can watch the tower. We're still out of sight.'

'I agree,' said Kali, which didn't surprise Fyn at all, but he did think they were right. He wanted to see what was going on just as much as they did.

They turned back to face the tower.

For a while nothing happened, but as Fyn was wondering if everything could go smoothly, a loud boom sounded out in the distance. Birds squawked and flapped loudly as they fled through the sky.

Henry Flame whined, cowering behind Fyn who leaned down to stroke him.

A second boom followed, then a third.

'I'm hoping that was part of the plan,' Amy said, her voice slightly shaken.

'That's just Mya,' said Kali.

'What do you mean?' Fyn asked.

'Sand bombs,' said Theo. 'It's a diversion. Loud but harmless. Come on. I want to see this.'

They started walking back, closer to the edge of the clearing, but the others were no longer there.

Before Fyn could wonder where they had gone, an alarm began to screech inside the tower.

'Damn!' Theo cursed. 'They'll be trapped! Any agents who left will come right back.'

It was worse. Five sets of neon-blue lights approached overhead. Soarers. Their gentle humming was barely audible over the alarm. They landed smoothly at the base of the tower, each carrying two agents.

'We can't let them go in!' said Theo.

'Wait!' said Fyn. 'We can't mess up the plan!'

'It's already ruined!' Theo argued. 'It's now or never! Kali?'

She spoke to Fyn and Amy. 'If we're captured, make sure our parents know we went out with a fight.'

Without another word she ran with Theo, out from the jungle and directly at the agents.

Daylight was arriving and, although frustrated, Fyn watched in awe as they got to work. They moved with speed, precision, and elegance. Already three agents were on the ground, but the element of surprise was quickly lost.

The seven remaining agents retaliated quickly, pulling the baton-type devices on their arms which blasted bright orange laser beams.

Theo and Kali narrowly avoided them, but instead of continuing to fight, they ran inside the tower.

The agents followed them, leaving their unconscious comrades behind.

'Let's take out the soarers,' said Fyn.

'What?' asked Amy. 'How?'

'No idea, but that's what the others were going to do.' He tied Henry Flame's vine to a tree trunk. 'Don't worry fella. We'll be back soon. Come on,' he said to Amy.

His pulse racing, he approached the nearest soarer. It was somewhere between the size of a large motorbike and a small car. Its neon-blue lights shone brightly in a series of tubes that criss-crossed around the shell of the machine.

A crash sounded above them in the tower.

'I don't think we have long!' said Amy. 'Wait! They're still *on*, right?'

'I don't know.' There was no fuel tank that Fyn could see, and no key or clear ignition point.

'Push them!'

'What?'

'They're not actually on the ground,' Amy explained. 'Look! They're hovering! Maybe we can move them!'

'You're right!' he said.

They pushed against the soarer. It didn't move as easily as he'd hoped, but it did move. It felt like it was held in place by a magnet. With effort, they managed to shift it to the back of the tower and hide it behind the tree line.

'Quick!' said Amy. 'Let's try some more!' She rushed over to another soarer.

A second crash sounded from inside the tower. People were shouting, but Fyn couldn't single out any one voice over the alarm. He reached Amy's side and helped her again.

They worked fast, ensuring to avoid the unconscious agents around them as they did. When they had moved all but the last soarer, laser beams shot out of a second-floor window, singeing the tree opposite.

Dimitry leapt out, swung down from a branch, and landed gracefully on the grass.

Immediately afterwards, a woman Fyn didn't recognise did the same.

More orange blasts streamed out after them.

He ducked behind the soarer, pulling Amy down with him.

Dimitry and the woman turned and ran to the entrance of the tower, charging back in.

'Are they mad?' Amy asked.

'I think it's everyone or no one!' said Fyn. 'Hurry! Let's move this soarer!'

'Hold on!' Mya ran out of the jungle, stooping low to the ground with her bow in hand. Her eyes frantically searched the area, and her hair was full of sand. 'I got caught by my own distraction,' she explained, 'but I took out some agents on the way. Where are the others?'

'Inside, I think,' said Fyn.

'We need to help them,' she replied. 'Look at this panel on the soarer.' She pointed to a shiny pad about the size of a dinner plate. 'It's how they fly them. Certain devices here read the energy of the person. Hold the palm of your hand on the panel and line up the soarer to face the entrance. When we're all outside, push the soarer towards it as hard as you can. It won't power down right away. Do you understand?'

'Yes,' said Fyn, although he wasn't quite sure.

She patted his shoulder, half-smiled at the pair of them, then ran to join the others inside.

'I wish we'd known it was that easy to move them!' Amy grumbled as she stood up again.

Careful not to climb on the soarer, Fyn pressed his hand to the panel. As soon as he touched it, he could feel it gently pulsing against his palm.

The soarer moved with no resistance, and they aligned it to the tower's entrance with ease. Moments later, Mya, Theo, and Kali rushed out.

'Be ready!' Mya shouted as she launched an arrow back somewhere into the tower.

Orange lasers shot from inside the entrance and two agents ran out.

Art was right behind them. He grabbed them by the scruffs of their necks and lifted them off the ground. Then he threw them into the clearing where they crashed in a heap.

Dimitry ran out next with the woman Fyn guessed was Florentina. Then came Scott.

'Now!' shouted Mya.

Fyn swiftly pulled his hand off the panel as Amy gave the soarer an almighty shove. This time it really soared – directly towards the entrance of the tower.

It was as though everything happened in slow motion. Everyone moved out of the way of the speeding soarer, their heads turning to the side to watch it whizz past them.

Mya stooped to grab one of the fallen agent's arms and pulled on the blaster. A burst of orange laser beams shot directly after the soarer as it sped into the tower. A ball of fire swept through the air as the soarer exploded.

Fyn was thrown backwards and the ground shook as the foundations of the tower were utterly destroyed. He looked up – vision blurry from the blast – and saw the building trying to hold steady, yet already beginning to collapse in a mass of wood, smoke, and flames. His ears were ringing, or was that still the alarm?

Scott grabbed him by the shoulders.

'Run!' he shouted. '*Run!*'

CHAPTER TWENTY-ONE

Parting Ways

Fyn managed to stand, then did his best to run with the others – out of the clearing and back into the jungle, as fast as his shaking legs could carry him. Ears ringing, he struggled to focus as he fumbled to free a panicking Henry Flame, then, together, they kept going as another explosion ripped across the sky behind them.

He did his best to follow Amy as she ran slightly ahead, the thought of agents bursting through the trees and chasing them down urging him on, but what had it cost to rescue Florentina?

It was supposed to have been a fairly simple mission. Instead, they'd blown up an agent base *and* been seen doing it. Other than marking themselves with bright flashing lights, he didn't know how they could have drawn more attention. He felt a stitch in his side but kept running. Distance from the tower was key.

After some time, as Fyn was beginning to wonder how much longer he could run, Scott brought them together in a huddle.

'Is everyone still with us?' he asked, puffing to catch his breath. He did a quick head count. 'Good. Florentina, I'm glad to see you. I hope they didn't put you through too much.'

Fyn kept looking behind. His hearing had returned to normal, but surely they weren't about to stop for a chat?

'Relax,' said Art, putting one hand on his shoulder. 'We made good ground. We can afford a moment.'

'Nothing I couldn't cope with,' Florentina replied to Scott. She had a gentle voice. 'They tried to break me but lost interest when they realised it was a waste of time.'

Dimitry grunted.

'Don't worry,' she said as she leaned into him. 'Just minor scratches. Plus, I got a few of them back on the way out. For the most part I was left alone.'

'Thank goodness,' said Mya.

'I'm sorry to push so soon,' said Scott, 'but—'

'—It's okay,' said Florentina. 'I was there for a reason.' She looked at them all, taking in the familiar and unfamiliar faces. Her gaze lingered on Fyn and Amy. She was shorter than Dimitry and slighter of frame. Her dark hair was shaved on her right side but flowed below her shoulder on her left. She looked tired but not defeated, and Fyn realised that despite what she had been through, she had no problem keeping up with them. She wasn't even out of breath.

'A few days ago,' she said, 'I overheard some agents. They'd been talking to others from the cells at the citadel and said a man from Rogan's village was there.'

'Daniel?' Scott asked.

'I can't be sure, but I assume so.'

Fyn's stomach leapt. He looked at Amy who smiled back.

'The citadel is at the very heart of the City of the Sea,' said Art. 'I cannot help but wonder if he was caught there or taken there?'

'At least we're one step closer to helping him,' said Scott encouragingly.

'I'm pleased,' said Dimitry, 'and trust this concludes our current business?'

'It does,' Scott replied. 'Thank you to both of you for your help.'

'You're welcome,' said Dimitry, 'and I wish you well in your adventures. When you find him,' he said to Fyn, 'I hope he is everything you could ask for after so long. Expectations can ring untrue, so try not to have any.'

'Thanks,' Fyn replied, slightly taken aback but grateful all the same.

'I hope we meet again,' said Florentina. 'It's been brief this time and I sense things are going to get very interesting for you.'

'*Going to?*' Fyn smiled.

Dimitry turned to go, but Florentina waited.

'Keep on this way,' she pointed, 'until you reach a river. We left a raft under a fallen bridge. It won't make your journey safer, but it will make it faster. It might not be the best thing for your furry friend though,' she added, looking at Henry Flame. 'Good luck.'

She walked a few paces with Dimitry, and together they vanished seamlessly into the jungle.

'I guess they're not the only ones to part ways,' Scott said, as Fyn began to wonder how Henry Flame would cope with a river.

Mya turned to Theo and Kali. 'You know what this means. Thank you for your help, but it's time for you to go back to Homehill. No detours. No chances. Update Rogan right away. The village could be in trouble if any of us were recognised.' She turned back to Scott. 'Are Fyn and Amy going with them?'

Fyn listened eagerly.

'No,' said Scott. 'I said I'd look after them. They're my responsibility.'

Fyn didn't think this was the answer she wanted, but she didn't argue.

'If Daniel is alive in a cell,' Theo said, raising his voice slightly, 'but our entire village could be in danger, why are we not *all* going back to help our home first? Daniel left us. He left *them*,' he glanced at Fyn and Amy. 'Maybe it's okay to leave *him* for a while. I mean all he does lately is abandon people.'

'Hey!' Fyn retaliated.

'Theo!' scolded Kali. 'You know that's not true! You should apologise.'

'Why?' Theo challenged. 'I wanted to rescue him. I still do, but home comes first.'

Fyn felt his face tighten and his teeth clamp together. He stared at Theo with a rage burning inside of him but somewhere deeper, as reluctant as he was to admit it, he understood where he was coming from.

His doubts began to resurface. Was it possible that his dad *had* abandoned the people of Homehill? What if he *could* have tried harder to come home? Could he simply be the kind of person to leave? Dimitry's parting words echoed in his mind. Were his expectations too high?

'Remember, Scott's family are waiting,' said Mya, 'and so is Bernie. No one is taking this decision lightly, but this is Daniel. He's Fyn's father and one of us. We have no idea why he was taken or what shape he could be in. We don't know...' She shook her head, refusing to accept whatever she'd been about to say.

Fyn imagined her next words... *How long he's got. If he's alive. How long there could be until catastrophe.*

It was true. If the agents had his dad, they could be using him right now, forcing him to help them unlock mysterious secrets which, according to Rogan, could weaken the lining between worlds and destroy everything. Another reminder that even if they did get him back, getting home wasn't guaranteed.

Theo stayed quiet.

'I hope we will see you again soon,' said Kali. Then surprisingly, she stepped forward and held Fyn's hands in hers. 'Be safe and be strong.'

She squeezed gently and smiled.

Amy raised her eyebrows.

'You too,' Fyn replied gratefully, a warm glow reaching up his arms. 'Please tell Grandad Bernie we're okay.'

'I will.'

'And send my family my love,' said Scott.

She nodded sincerely. 'We'll look after them all – your family, and Bernie. Won't we, Theo?'

He rolled his eyes, but his voice was kinder as he replied, 'Yes.'

'Thanks,' said Fyn.

Theo and Kali turned to leave.

'Wait!' Fyn called. He sighed, looking from Amy down to Henry Flame.

'What is it?' asked Kali.

'Can you please take him with you? Back to Grandad Bernie?'

'But...' said Amy, frowning.

'He can't stay with us,' said Fyn. 'It's not safe. You heard what Florentina said about the river.'

She nodded. 'Just make sure they know he's not a demon.'

'We will,' Theo replied.

Fyn crouched down and stroked Henry Flame behind the ears. 'I'm sorry to leave you. I've loved having you around. It's just better to go with them. You'll be safer that way.'

Henry Flame looked up with his big orange eyes and tilted his head. He looked so gentle – so understanding.

Kali walked over and let Henry Flame sniff her hand before she took the vine lead. 'He'll be with your Grandad Bernie in no time.'

Fyn did his best to smile but didn't feel happy.

As they left, Henry Flame kept looking back.

'Go on,' Fyn urged, but it wasn't easy to say goodbye or leave behind someone else he cared about.

CHAPTER TWENTY-TWO

Washed Away

Trekking in the direction Florentina had advised, the lack of agents was as welcoming as it was unnerving.

Fyn pressed his palm and sighed, remembering where the vine had rubbed against it when walking Henry Flame.

Amy stayed at his side in silence, while Mya, Art, and Scott kept just ahead.

After a short time he heard water flowing and they reached the edge of the trees at the bank of a wide river.

Downstream was what remained of an old wooden bridge. It looked like it had collapsed long ago, with only its foundations still standing.

They approached steadily, keeping under the shade of the trees.

Mya crept into the open. Sneaking out to the remains, she disappeared down the riverbank, emerging soon afterwards to signal them to join her.

Florentina had been right. A large raft awaited them by the water's edge. It was made of thick, dry bamboo and there were two long wooden poles next to it.

'It's in good shape,' Art said, checking it all over.

'How are we going to do this?' asked Mya. 'Wait until dark or take the risk now?'

'I don't think we can wait,' said Scott. 'I'm surprised the agents aren't everywhere already. We need to keep going as fast as we can.'

'Hopefully if they do see us,' said Fyn, 'they won't know we're the ones they're after.'

'True,' said Amy. 'I mean, there aren't as many of us now.'

'They'll question anyone they find,' said Mya. 'They may have expected us to separate.'

'So we go,' said Art.

He lifted the raft with Mya and Scott, before wading into the water to hold it steady as they lowered it in.

'It would be best for Amy and Fyn to climb on first and stay in the middle,' Mya suggested. 'Scott and I can take a paddle stick on either side by the front. With you in the middle at the back,' she added to Art, 'hopefully we'll balance out.'

'Agreed,' said Scott, reaching out to Fyn. 'Here. Let me help you.'

Fyn took his hand and stepped onto the raft. He wobbled as it tilted beneath his feet while Art continued to hold it in place.

Scott helped Amy on next, and the cold water splashed up at them as the raft bobbed with the current.

Despite the circumstances, Fyn felt a thrill of excitement as Mya and Scott worked to push them away from the shore with the paddle sticks.

'How far do we need to go?' asked Amy.

'As far as we can manage before the coast,' said Mya. 'If we reach the sea, I expect we'll be spotted quickly so we'll stop before then.'

Mya and Scott gave a last heave and successfully pushed the raft further out into the river.

The change was immediate. The current became much stronger and speedily carried them away, the foundations of the broken bridge fading out of sight behind them.

With the wind flowing through his hair and the water splashing all around him, Fyn nearly forgot they were on the run. He felt truly alive.

They moved with the bumps of the current, but Mya had planned it well and their balance was evenly spread. She and Scott had a steady rhythm in steering the raft and keeping it centred.

Fyn looked out to the high riverbanks, where dry tangled bushes and thin branches stretched over the river. A yellow snake hung its coils from a branch not more than twenty metres away, but that too was soon behind them in the distance.

He looked to the sky, and a shiver ran down his spine as he remembered the soarers. There was nowhere to hide.

'How are you finding things on Eromlos?' Art asked from the back of the raft, successfully distracting him.

Fyn shimmied around to face him and Amy.

'I know it's been a lot to take in since you arrived,' Art continued, 'but beyond that?'

Fyn thought about it. So much had changed in the last few hours alone. Things felt more dangerous now, but he considered life back home. He'd always had this weight over him as he wondered if he'd ever find his dad. Even though, thanks to Theo, he had fresh doubts, it did feel better to know answers were coming, even with agents after them. 'I don't know,' he said at last. 'It's kind of crazy at times. It's not easy, but there are things I prefer.'

'Same,' said Amy. 'If I forget about getting home, there is something about it here where I feel a bit freer if that makes sense? Everything's so busy where we come from. It's always one thing after another. At least it's the school holidays though. This would all feel so much worse if we had school to deal with too.'

'What's school?' asked Art.

'You're kidding right?' Amy asked, but he looked back at her straight-faced.

'It's like this prison for children,' she explained, and Fyn laughed. 'They give you all this pressure, make you wear the same clothes, and tell you it's a good thing to prepare you for being a grown up.'

'Amy...' Scott said from the front.

'Oh okay, I'm just kidding.' She smiled. 'Sort of. School is where we go to learn. It's not really *that* bad, but there can be a lot of pressure sometimes.'

'You won't find pressure here,' said Mya sarcastically, but her lips twitched, and Fyn was glad to see her relax a little.

'If you took away the agents, I think I'd really like it here,' he said. 'It would be better to know we can get back home, but apart from that it's exciting.' He looked around again. 'We have rainforests on our Earth, and there are places you can go on safari to see things like elephants and giraffes, but not anywhere close to where we live.'

'What are *je-raffs?*' asked Art.

Scott grinned as he continued to steer the raft. 'Good question! Let's just say they're so tall they can eat from the treetops when standing on the ground.'

'Like giant long necks?' Art asked.

'I guess there are similarities,' said Scott, 'but they're not birds. They're yellow-and-brown mammals.'

Mya looked impressed as she continued to steer the raft. 'That's something I'd enjoy seeing. What else is different?'

'Well, where we come from,' said Amy, 'people can use technology. Everyone has access to it.'

'At least everyone with access is allowed to use it,' said Fyn. 'There are still lots of places where people don't have the basics – even things like food and water.'

'I wonder if there are worlds where that's not the case,' pondered Mya.

'Hopefully many,' said Scott.

'I have wondered what other worlds are like for a long time,' said Art as they continued to bob along the river. 'I've asked Scott and Daniel about it but there are so many possibilities. I love the idea of it. There could be a world for anything.'

'Like a world with a purple sky,' said Amy.

'Or a world full of cyborg dinosaurs,' said Fyn.

Art chuckled. 'I suppose anything is possible, but I'm not sure what *they* are.'

'Far too complicated to explain,' said Scott. 'Although I forgot how much I can miss things where I come from. There were a lot of good times. Did you know I was there the day you were born?' he asked Fyn.

'No!' Fyn replied. 'I had no idea. Are you serious?'

'Absolutely! I remember driving Daniel to the hospital from work. He was so excited, there is no way he could have done it himself.' He laughed. 'I'll have to visit someday – after we get you home.'

Fyn smiled at the thought. A world where he could have his family together and Scott could still be in their lives.

Things went quiet for a while that, with everyone either lost in thought or keeping watch. The riverbanks became more of the same. The jungle was truly enormous.

'Uh-oh,' said Mya. 'Incoming!'

Fyn looked up. Five soarers were approaching from the distance. Three were like the ones he'd seen before, but two were larger. He could see agents leaning out the side of them.

'Steady up everyone,' she said. 'Art. Scott. Ready?' She looked over her shoulder at them.

Art gave a stiff nod.

'Stay in the middle of the raft,' said Scott to Fyn and Amy. 'Be prepared to take our paddle sticks if things escalate.'

'"*If* things escalate,"' said Amy. 'I mean come on...'

The soarers hovered above the river ahead of them, maintaining a steady distance as the raft continued to flow downstream. They held formation in a row with a smaller soarer on each end and another in the middle. An announcement sounded from the middle soarer – like the one they'd heard during the raid at Homehill.

'Steer the raft to the shore and wait until we detain you. If you do not comply, we will fire.'

Fyn and Amy looked at each other nervously.

'Play dumb for a minute,' said Scott. He gestured to the soarers, raising his arms as though he didn't understand.

'Steer the raft to the shore and wait until we detain you,' the announcement repeated more forcefully. 'If you do not comply, we will fire. We will not ask again.'

Scott, Mya, and Art didn't move.

'What are you doing?' asked Amy, but Mya held out a hand to silence her.

Fyn looked ahead and thought he realised why.

The soarers began to move towards them with their familiar hum as they kept their height above the river. The current became more turbulent as they flew directly over the top of them, increasing the wind around the raft on their way.

'It's not over yet,' said Art.

Still in formation, the soarers turned again to face them but this time from behind.

'Hold tight!' said Scott. 'It's about to get wild!'

Fyn saw the current frothing and churning around rocks as the river ahead took a drastic dip on a slope.

Then they hit the rapids.

He tried to grasp the ropes that held the raft together and gripped his sandals between the bamboo, but the raft was slippery, and he soon became sore from the effort of hanging on.

Behind him, the two larger soarers were lowering their blasters.

'Now!' shouted Mya, then she, Art, and Scott pulled out familiar-looking batons from their slings. They had agent weapons!

'When did...?' Fyn started.

'Back at the tower,' Scott replied. 'We thought they may come in handy but kept them switched off to avoid being tracked! Here, take this!' He passed his paddle stick to Fyn as Mya passed Amy hers.

It was amazing news, but Fyn didn't feel confident against five soarers and all the agents they carried. He watched as the soarers flew closer.

'You have been warned,' came a final announcement.

Two huge laser beams shot from the larger soarers and hit the water around the raft.

'Duck!' shouted Mya.

The other soarers opened fire, as did Scott, Mya, and Art.

Orange laser blasts filled the sky.

Fyn threw himself down as one hit his paddle stick and knocked it from his hands into the river.

They sailed on, now out of control.

'Watch out!' yelled Scott.

The raft lifted against a rock, scraped over the top of it, and splashed back into the water.

Fyn started to lose track of which way was up. With every crash he ached more and more from holding on. Another blast dashed past his head, this time singeing his hair.

One of Art's shots hit home.

The soarer in the middle veered to the side and crashed into the larger soarer on the right. They both lost control and span into the river behind them. The remaining three soarers changed formation, one smaller soarer on each side of the bigger one.

'We can't stay out in the open like this!' shouted Art. 'We need cover. They can't fly their soarers through the forest.'

'We can't steer!' said Mya, firing up at the large soarer. 'We have to make it through the rapids!'

'Just keep holding—'

Scott's sentence was cut short as a blast from one of the agents hit him square in the chest.

'No!' screamed Fyn, but there was nothing he could do. He saw Scott's eyes close, and his body fall limply into the water where the current swept him into a rock and beneath the surface.

Fyn felt his whole body lurch as the raft tilted steeply and he fell with the others into the cold force of the river.

Chapter Twenty-Three
Lost Together

Fyn sank into the depths of the water. With every effort he could muster up he held his breath and tried furiously to swim back to the surface as the current pulled him further below.

Must hold on! he urged himself, desperately struggling to kick his legs in the right direction. If only he could take just one more breath of fresh air. His chest felt like it was going to burst.

He couldn't see where he was going. All he could make out were thick, frothy rapids rushing around and over him. His foot hit something – the riverbed. He pressed his feet down, feeling the ground scrape beneath his sandals, then bent his knees and pushed with everything he had. He breached the surface and drew in what must have been the biggest breath he'd taken in his life. Then he was dragged right back under.

He tried to keep track of the light – that was his route to safety. Maybe the air in his lungs would help him float if he stayed steady. He resurfaced and gasped in another breath, frantically trying to look around. Rocks were everywhere. It took everything he had not to crash into them ... like Scott had.

He quickly took another deep breath then was pulled back under, this time for longer. Panic built within him – the fear that he wouldn't make it back to the surface. What if he ran out of time? His body craved oxygen. He forced himself to keep his mouth shut and not seek air where he knew there was none.

When he reached the surface again it was with relief. The rapids were finally easing and there was no sign of the soarers. He continued to tread water, trying to get his bearings and spot anyone else.

'Fyn!'

He span his head to the right and saw Mya pulling herself out of the water and onto the riverbank. Art was knelt beside her with ... Amy! She was lying in his arms as he lowered her gently to the ground.

Fyn swam towards them with renewed energy. Finding his feet a little downstream, he trudged through the water – trying not to lose his sandals in the mud. Once on shore he ran hard to them, ignoring the way his waterlogged clothes slapped against his skin and stuck to him.

'Her leg is bleeding,' he started, but then Amy spluttered out a cough of water and inhaled deeply.

'She's okay, Fyn. She's okay,' said Mya leaning forward, her hands on her knees.

'I'm not putting in the effort,' Amy rasped, 'to come to another universe, only to let some river get the best of me.' She smiled but looked tired. 'It was close though,' she admitted before coughing some more.

'Your leg?' Fyn asked.

'It's fine,' she said. 'I just hit a rock is all.'

'Let me see that,' said Mya as Art stepped back to give them some room.

'Where are the agents?' Fyn asked. 'Where is Scott?'

Mya's face was solemn.

'Where's Scott?' he asked again.

'We lost him, Fyn.'

He heard her but didn't listen, instead pacing to the water's edge, looking out as far as he could.

'We lost him,' she repeated, moving away from Amy and towards him.

'No,' he said simply, unwilling to accept what she was saying. 'How can we lose him?'

She stared at him without speaking as he felt the answer creep over him like a fever. Scott had been blasted in the chest, fallen into the river, and smashed against a rock. How could he have survived?

'Maybe he washed up further down the river?' He started walking back to the spot he had swam ashore.

'*Please* stop, Fyn,' she pleaded.

He wanted to challenge. He wanted to shout. 'We need to keep searching!' he urged.

'He could be anywhere. Downstream or the other side of the river. We can hope he made it, but we can't waste time looking.'

'How is that a waste of time?' he asked. 'He has a family! He's part of our group!' He held himself back from saying the rest. He was their friend. Being with him made him feel closer to his dad than he had in years.

'I care too,' said Mya, her voice cracking, 'I do, but we cannot stay out in the open like this. Not with the agents so close. The only thing I want to believe is he's okay. If he is ... he'll find us. We have to trust that.'

'What if he isn't?' Fyn asked.

'He wouldn't want you looking for him,' said Art. 'He wouldn't want any of us risking ourselves.'

Fyn looked to Amy. Surely she would support him.

Her eyes gave her away.

He stared at the river. He knew the longer they waited, the more vulnerable they became.

'Fyn.' Amy stood slightly behind him.

'I know,' he said, defeat washing over him. 'I just...'

'I know too,' she said back. 'You don't need to explain – unless you want to.'

They walked together then, the four of them. Away from the river that had seemed so exciting a short time ago, and into the jungle he was beginning to tire of. The sunlight dimmed again.

'What about Marina and the kids?' he asked, thinking out loud and dreading the answer.

Mya paused ahead of him but didn't look back. 'We'll get word to them as soon as we can. They'll assume he's safe. Hopefully he will be by the time it comes to that.'

'Assuming they're okay too,' said Amy.

She didn't reply.

Fyn thought of Grandad Bernie and the way he always knew what to say to make him feel better. He thought of the villagers at Homehill and how he hoped they were safe too. Then he thought of his mum and how much he wanted to make it back to her. They had to find his dad.

As they trekked on, Fyn's clothes gradually dried from soaking wet to damp, and when they stopped in a patch of clear sunlight, he and Amy sat together to sort through their things as Mya and Art stepped aside to discuss plans.

'I lost most of what was in my sling in the river,' Amy said. 'Not that it's important compared to everything else.'

'I know what you mean,' he replied. 'I don't have much left either, but I *do* still have these...' He pulled out a wet paper bag and peeled some of it away to reveal a few jelly sweets.

'How have you kept *those* secret?' Amy exclaimed.

He shrugged. 'I was saving them. Help yourself.'

She shook her head in disbelief but took one right away. She popped it in her mouth and let her head tilt back as she enjoyed the sugary rush.

He ate a few himself and then asked, 'How are you? You know, after cutting your leg and nearly drowning.'

'All in a day's work,' she replied. Then she said honestly, 'I'm trying. Mya put herby paste on the cut, and it feels fine, but I'm not sure how *I* am. I can't stop thinking about Scott and his family. Poor little Rosie won't understand at all and...' she faltered.

'What is it?' he asked.

'...I kind of don't want to say. You already have so much to think about.'

'It's okay,' he said. 'I mean yes, there *is* a lot to think about, but my stuff doesn't stop me being there for your stuff. We're besties remember?'

She smiled gratefully. 'Thanks.'

'So, what is it?' he asked.

'I absolutely want to support you, and I do, and I will,' she started.

'I know,' he replied, wondering what was coming.

'It's just, when we were back at Grandad Bernie's house and Martin came at us, there wasn't really any time to think.'

'It was madness,' he said, remembering how things were in the moment.

'Exactly, and the thing is, we leapt through the world window without knowing what we were doing…'

He waited for her to continue.

'…and now, well to be honest I'm kind of scared,' she admitted.

'That makes sense,' he said, trying to be supportive. 'There's a lot going on.'

'No, it's not that,' she replied. 'I can cope with what's happening here – at least I think I can. It's more that I'm worried… Worried we might not make it home. I know we're all feeling that way,' she added quickly, 'but I didn't expect all this to happen, and I can't help it… I feel guilty, because there's a part of me that wonders if I should have stayed home. I'm worried I won't see my family again.' She looked down at the ground in shame.

'Hey,' he said, feeling bad for her and grateful at the same time. 'You have nothing to feel guilty about. If anything, it's my fault you're stuck here.'

'How is this your fault?' she asked. 'You didn't make this happen. We did what we had to do, and I know that really. I guess I'm just feeling all meh about it since Scott, well, you know...' She looked at him apologetically.

Inside he felt tired and defeated, but he didn't want to show that to Amy.

'Fyn?'

'It's okay to feel that way,' he said as confidently as he could, 'but Scott might have made it, and we know where my dad is. We have to keep hope. You can *always* talk to me.'

'Alright,' she replied more certainly. 'Hopefully Scott's okay. We'll find your dad. We'll return to Grandad Bernie *and* Henry Flame, and then we'll get home.'

'Exactly!' He gave her a friendly nudge on the arm, and despite the heaviness of the situation, they shared a tiny moment of calm as Mya and Art returned and sat next to them.

'We lost our weapons to the river,' Mya stated, her words immediately weighing Fyn down again, 'and we have low supplies. We have to go with what we know.'

'What's that?' he asked tentatively.

'The agents *will* be coming. They'll assume we survived the river, and it's too much to hope they didn't see either of you on the raft.'

'What are you saying?' he asked.

'It's only a matter of time before they find us again,' said Art. 'When they do, you have to let us take the fall.'

'What?' asked Fyn and Amy together. 'Why?'

'There's no use in the four of us getting caught,' said Mya. 'There's no way we'll free Daniel that way.'

'So we're supposed to let you get captured?' Fyn asked. He couldn't believe his ears.

'We stick together,' she replied, 'and if at any point the agents are close, the two of you have to hide. No drawing attention to yourselves. If they ask, we'll try to convince them we lost you to the river.'

'But...' he started.

'...and no arguments,' she finished.

CHAPTER TWENTY-FOUR

The Creature

'There go some more,' said Amy quietly, as they watched blue streaks zoom across the darkening sky between gaps in the treetops.

'The agents are out in force tonight,' said Mya, as she held back a branch for them to walk by. 'No doubt they'll be on the ground too.'

Fyn remained silent. The idea that he and Amy might need to let Mya and Art get captured wasn't the only thing getting to him; it was also the agents in general. He found himself wondering how they got away with what they did, and how they would feel if it was the other way around. He tripped on a root and scowled.

'How did it get to be like this?' he asked. 'How did the agents take over?'

'Good questions,' said Mya. 'I imagine they started small and spread like a disease. Now they have the power, and no one knows how to take it back.'

'I'd help if I knew how,' said Fyn.

'Maybe you already are,' said Art.

The thought was comforting.

They reached a large rock face rising above them in the forest. At its base was the mouth of a shadow-filled cave.

Fyn couldn't see beyond a few steps inside.

'I've not seen this place before,' said Mya thoughtfully. 'Wait here.' She disappeared into the darkness.

'She's crazy,' said Amy.

'She's done worse,' whispered Art.

'I'm not sure that makes it better,' Fyn replied.

'You know I *can* hear you?' Mya's voice echoed from inside the cave. She returned and placed her sling on the floor. 'It's an ideal place to settle for the night. Plus, unless I'm mistaken, there's water over there.'

Fyn followed her gaze to the surface of a pool reflecting moonlight behind some trees.

'Could you please check?' she asked him.

Glad for some space, he accepted. 'Amy?'

'Let's go,' she replied.

'See if it's cloudy, smells bad, or has a layer of scum on top,' said Mya. 'If it's fresh, maybe we can use it tomorrow. We'll set things up here.'

'All those times we used to talk about adventures,' said Amy as they reached the edge of the pool. 'I never imagined this.'

'Me neither,' Fyn replied absentmindedly. He couldn't shift the thought that something seemed familiar.

'And I don't even want to think about what could be in that water,' she added while staring down at it. 'At least it doesn't smell. Hey, have you noticed it's really quiet?'

'I guess,' he mumbled, still trying to figure out what was on his mind.

'No. I mean it's *really* quiet,' she pressed. 'Listen... I can't hear anything.'

She was right. All the jungle sounds he had learned to tune out were gone. No insects. No birds. No anything other than the gentle trickling of the water that fed into and out of the pool.

'What do you think changed?' he asked, feeling wary and trying to keep his voice quieter than before.

'Agents?' suggested Amy.

'I hope not.'

'Likewise. I can't hear the others either, but ... I think ... I *can* hear something...'

Fyn heard a rustling sound in the distance, approaching them so rapidly it soon sounded more like it was crashing through the forest.

'Hey!'

Fyn nearly jumped out of his skin. It was Mya from behind them. She hadn't spoken loudly but it was enough to catch him off guard.

'Did you hear...' he began to ask.

'No time,' she interrupted. 'Get in the pool and hide. Don't make a sound. Quickly!' She turned and quietly ran back to the cave.

'Oh, man,' said Amy. 'I'm not ready for this.'

Fyn held a finger to his lips.

She nodded as the crashing sound became even louder.

They looked at each other wide-eyed then waded into the water with their slings still on their backs.

It was the last thing he wanted to do. He'd had more than enough of being wet for one day but didn't want to think about the alternative.

They moved further in, every step harder to take than the last.

The crashing sound continued to get louder, and just when their shoulders dipped beneath the water and the surrounding reeds covered their faces, it stopped.

The trickling pool seemed as loud as a roaring wave.

Not daring to move, they waited.

Seconds felt like forever, and Fyn's ears pricked at a peculiar new sound – like that of a dog lapping up water.

He lifted his feet, unplugging them from the mud they'd settled in, and carefully peered through a gap in the reeds to the source of the sound. His mouth fell open in a silent gasp and he fought the urge to grab Amy and try to run.

On the other side of the pool, a creature unlike anything he'd seen before was stooped down and drinking with a thick snake-like tongue, sending ripples across its reflection in the water. Its dark body was almost human in form, with four limbs and a torso, but each limb was very long, very thin, and extremely muscular. The position it held itself in made its arms and legs look like they were bent the wrong way, and it appeared to be covered in scales.

Fyn stared at its tall pointed ears, then at its crocodile-like jaw which was easily the length of one of his arms.

He forced himself to look to Amy. She, too, was staring at it in fear.

They bent their knees to sink lower into the pool.

He hated it as the water covered his neck, then his chin. Lowering his mouth beneath the surface he felt sick as he flashed back to the river. Then Amy spluttered like water had gone up her nose.

He looked at her in alarm as the lapping sound stopped.

She forced herself to quietness, but it was short-lived. She lifted her mouth out of the water and coughed loudly, yet apologetically.

The creature stared intently at the reeds they were hiding in. It tilted its head, flickering its long tongue as though tasting the air around it. Then it flashed its sharp teeth.

Its legs bent oddly with each step as it crept around the edges of the pool. It was being stealthy. *No*, Fyn realised. It was hunting. Worse – it was hunting *them*.

As it got closer, the reeds started to hide it from view.

Fyn flinched as a branch snapped from behind them. Then he watched in horror as a claw-like finger parted the reeds above Amy. Staring straight back at him was a wide yellow eye, slit from top to bottom by a thick black pupil.

'Get away from them!'

The creature span away to face Art who was running at it. It let out a fearsome roar.

'Over here!' shouted Mya from the other side of the pool.

The creature span back to face her. It stood on its two hind legs, stretched its arms to the side, and lowered itself into a strange twisted position.

'It's going to pounce!' called Fyn, lifting his head back out of the water.

The creature whipped around to face him.

He lowered himself back down, trying to hide again, then several neon-blue lights flashed across the sky, stopping above them all.

Cords fell to the ground and agents descended.

The creature leapt directly at one of them, sinking its teeth into an arm. The man screamed in pain as he fell.

The other agents fired, their lasers lighting the darkness. More struck at the creature as additional agents ran out of the trees.

The creature roared again, more ferociously than before, and leapt to the trunk of a tree. It climbed with ease, then leapt to another, and another, crashing away through the jungle and into the darkness.

Two agents ran to help the injured agent who was curled up in pain. The others directed their blasters at Mya and Art.

'Do not move,' said the agent closest to Art. She pushed something on to their backs and red energy bands sprung out, wrapping their arms tightly to their chests.

Mya and Art didn't speak.

'We think they're alone,' said another agent. 'We found these by a cave over there.' He held up their travel slings.

Fyn watched anxiously as the agents searched the area, but they didn't check the reeds where he and Amy remained hidden. Instead, they attached Mya and Art to the cords and signalled for them to be lifted into the air.

On the verge of rushing out to help, Fyn caught Art's eye and remembered his words, *Let us take the fall*.

More soarers arrived to collect the agents, and within minutes they were gone.

Fyn and Amy were alone.

CHAPTER TWENTY-FIVE

The Great Path

In the dark, Fyn and Amy had kept going as best they could, each carrying a fallen stick in an unsuccessful attempt to feel safer. Amy hadn't helped by pointing out that if the creature was to come again, they'd likely hear it crashing through the trees first. Then she had shuddered and added, '...unless we come across one on our way.' Even now in the light of day, the thought made Fyn uneasy.

'What do you think happened to everyone else?' she asked, sounding as tired as he felt. They had stopped to sit on some mossy rocks for a rest.

'I guess Theo and Kali will be well on their way back with Henry Flame,' he considered. 'They'll tell Rogan and the others we're okay.'

She raised an eyebrow.

'Well, they don't know about Scott,' he said, 'or the others, or us. If they're okay, at least it's good news for them. I don't want to stress out Grandad Bernie.'

'Me neither,' she replied, and he felt a rush of affection for her.

'Mya and Art are most likely locked up by now,' he continued, 'and I expect the agents are questioning them.'

'I hate to think about it!' she said. 'You never know though – they might be with your dad.'

His spirits lifted slightly. 'I hope so. It would be easier for us, but I wouldn't keep them together if it were up to me.'

He looked up. 'I think this is a good one. It looks easier to climb.'

They had been keeping an eye out for a tall and sturdy tree so Fyn could climb up and check they were still going in the right direction.

'We can always wait to find higher ground again?' Amy suggested. 'You know there's no way *I'm* going up.'

'It's okay,' said Fyn. 'I don't mind.'

She held out her hand. 'Watch out for agents.'

He handed her his sling and dusted himself off before starting to climb.

He was relieved to be right. It *was* a good tree, and it didn't take him long to reach the branches. He glanced down at the ground and saw Amy staring up at him, holding the trunk as though supporting a ladder.

He felt giddy. It was higher than he had realised and the rocks they'd just been sitting on looked more like pebbles to him now.

Breathing slowly, he turned his attention back to the tree, willing himself to ignore everything else. He wanted to call down to Amy and tell her he needed a minute but thought better of making the noise, so he steadied himself and kept going. It was easier once in the flow of it and he soon poked his head up into the clear sky, letting the fresh air fill his lungs. Settling on a sturdy branch, he wedged his feet against the tree trunk and took in the view.

The jungle stretched ahead, but in the distance he saw a great golden dome surrounded by elegant towers near the coast. It had to be the City of the Sea.

He marvelled at it, then after enjoying another breath of fresh air, started the descent down to update Amy.

'What did you see? Was there anything exciting?' she asked.

'I think there may have been a tree or two,' Fyn teased.

The next few days were long and tiring. Fyn climbed a tree a day and knew they were very close to the city now, but whenever he climbed up, he started to dread climbing back down. He relished every moment he could spend with a different view, and the city began to fascinate him. The closer to it they got, the clearer he saw the details. Lights were ascending and descending the towers, and soarers regularly flew into and out of the surrounding area.

In an attempt to take the scary edge off talking about the creature, they'd decided to name it Sally. It was a good tactic during the day, but not so much at night when they took turns keeping watch. Nights were definitely the toughest times, sitting up alone and listening for anything which could be out there, although sometimes the idea of silence was worse – especially knowing what may follow it.

In the daytime they often found themselves considering their next steps, hoping they'd be able to walk into the city like they would any other place, but they had no idea how they'd reach the cells and rescue the others.

Fyn imagined his mum and what she'd say, mid-chew on the end of a pencil, *One step at a time, Fyn. Everything leads to something*. Then he thought of Scott and was determined to see through what they'd started.

It was mid-afternoon on another sunny day when they reached a wide stone path which split the jungle. It stretched far to their left and their right, curving off out of sight at either end. The open space was so inviting, and Fyn had to resist the urge to leap out and sprint around to stretch his legs. Instead, they stayed under the cover of the trees but followed the path to their right, in the direction of the city.

As the afternoon wore on, they saw people on the path, travelling in the opposite direction. All had a similar bedraggled appearance. Several travelled with carts drawn by some kind of cattle, but they only carried blankets, empty sacks, or tired-looking passengers. He and Amy stayed well out of sight, hiding whenever anyone passed.

'Look!' said Fyn when he finally saw the entrance to the City of the Sea. Still a little way off, he could see a large archway surrounded by an opalescent wall at least twenty feet high, shimmering in the sunlight.

The towers behind it were visible over the walls, ranging in height, with several spectacularly spiralling into the sky. He could see now that the lights he had watched moving up and down them were platforms, and he was amazed to see people using them as lifts. In the middle of it all was the great golden dome. More platforms extended out from it, looping around in the perfect combination of grace and complexity.

Keeping under cover of the trees, they continued to approach the wall.

A group of people surrounded agents and a large soarer by the archway. The agents appeared to be checking them in and out of the city across a blue bridge formed of solid light. Fyn wondered if that was what the platforms in the city were made of.

Amy grabbed him and pulled him back.

'I can see them,' he whispered, eyeing the agents.

'Not *them*. That!'

He'd been paying so much attention to the agents he hadn't realised he'd run out of ground. They were at the edge of a ravine which dropped steeply to the sea and separated the city from the rest of the mainland. Small waterfalls poured from the rock face opposite them and crashed to the frothy waters below.

He mouthed a quiet 'thanks' to her, and she shook her head as though he really ought to have been paying attention to where he was going.

Observing the various people continue to leave the city empty-handed, they waited patiently through the rest of the afternoon and into the evening.

It was as the sun began to set that the first major change happened. No one had entered the city for hours, and now no one was leaving. The agents signalled to others inside the city walls and the bridge disappeared. Then they boarded their soarer and flew across the ravine and out of sight.

The archway lit up as an energy barrier flashed across the entrance.

Fyn sighed. 'How on Earth are we going to get in there?'

'How on *Eromlos*, you mean?' Amy corrected him.

He gave her his best *really* face.

'How about giving the Trojan horse technique a go?' she suggested.

'What? Disguise ourselves and be welcomed in? That sounds too obvious, and we don't have anything to hide in.'

'We have to give something a try.'

'I'm not exactly planning on sitting here forever,' he said. 'Maybe we should check the other side of the path.'

With no one in sight, half tiptoeing, and half running, they dashed across the path into the jungle on the other side. After a quick look around, it became apparent that it was much the same, but they could now see that the ravine completely cut the city off from the mainland.

Fyn groaned but didn't get any time to think on it as a gruff-sounding voice called from the path.

'Is someone there?'

There was nowhere else to go. He froze next to Amy at the edge of the cliff.

CHAPTER TWENTY-SIX

Petros and Zara

The gruff-sounding voice called again. 'If there's anyone there, show yourself.' It was a man.

Amy shook her head at Fyn.

He heard footsteps. Whoever it was, they were coming in after them. If they walked much further, they'd be spotted for sure.

'I mean you no harm,' said the man.

'Agents would never say that,' he said quietly to Amy. Then he called to him, 'What do you want?'

The footsteps stopped.

'Who are you?' Fyn asked.

'Just a traveller from the east,' came the reply.

'We are travelling from north of here,' Fyn called back, immediately annoying himself by sharing that he was with someone else. 'We mean no harm either but want to be left alone.' He waited and hoped his abruptness hadn't come across the wrong way.

'I understand,' the man replied, 'but you sound young, and us travellers should stick together. If you find yourself in need, just come to the edge of the path and ask for Petros. That's me. At the moment it's only my partner and myself there.'

'Thank you,' said Fyn, before gratefully hearing him retreat.

'What if he tells anyone we're here?' asked Amy.

'Do you think he would?' Fyn replied.

She shrugged. '*I* would, but he doesn't know how many of us there are. If things don't feel right we can always pretend people are waiting for us.'

In agreement, they walked back to the path.

A worn-looking and heavily bearded man was tending to a fire, next to an equally tired-looking woman. One of the cattle-like creatures they'd seen earlier rested behind them with a cart full of fruit and vegetables.

'There you are, young sir,' called the bearded man Fyn assumed was Petros. 'Don't be shy. There's nothing to fear. Come and join us by the fire. You must admit it's not as warm at night, especially by the sea. You too,' he called to Amy. 'Come on over, young lady.'

They moved closer to the fire.

The woman made room for them by shuffling over. She smiled welcomingly, but Fyn hesitated when he noticed several of her teeth were missing.

'Don't let the way we look put you off,' she said. 'I might look like an old crone, but I'd like to think I'm not one.'

'That's what *she* says!' the man chimed in cheerfully.

'Hush your trap, Petros!' she barked back.

'I'm sorry,' Fyn said. 'It wasn't that.'

'You're just a bit cautious, I'm sure,' she replied. 'That's wise. You never know who's out to get you in these parts.'

Petros laughed. 'Don't scare them!'

Fyn tried to smile but didn't quite know what to make of them. He moved closer to the fire with Amy, and they both sat down.

'There, that's better,' said the woman. 'I'm Zara, by the way. He's Petros. It's a pleasure to meet you.' She leaned over and held out her hand to Fyn and Amy.

They each shook it warily.

'There we are! We're all friends here,' said Zara, settling back again.

Petros saluted them with one arm while poking a stick into the fire with the other. 'It's quite unusual to catch two people your age out around here, so close to the city.'

'Why's that?' Fyn asked, looking at him with interest.

'Ha!' Petros laughed again. '"Why's that?" he asks! You two really aren't from around here, are you? No, no. Please forgive my cheek. It's as I said before; us regular folk need to stick together.'

'Precisely!' said Zara, patting her knees heavy-handedly.

'I'll start again,' said Petros. 'Zara and I are travelling from a village several days to the east of here called Farfields. I'm afraid we're here because it's the way of things. The morgoons in that city—'

'—Language, Petros!' Zara interrupted.

'Oh, don't you language me!' he moaned. 'I wouldn't say it in front of the young'uns if it meant worse than "idiots"! I'm telling our story!'

'Tell it nicely then,' she said matter-of-factly.

He frowned. 'Fine! The power-hungry *maniacs* in that city,' he said pointedly, 'demand all the local villages provide them with regular crops and supplies in order to "maintain the peace". I'll tell you now, I hate the lot of them for the constant disruption to our lives. Who they think they are, bossing us around the way they do, is beyond me!'

'Calm down, dear,' said Zara, patting her hand softly on his arm. She looked at Fyn and Amy in amusement. 'Honestly, we're no fans of the people in that place, but we do what we can because it's easier than the alternative. We make the trip once every twenty days. A few days here and a few days back. Then we get about two weeks to ourselves in return.'

'To ourselves, except we spend the time getting ready for the next trip,' Petros complained.

'That's awful!' said Amy, clenching her jaw and shaking her head. 'That sort of thing *really* gets to me.'

'It sounds like you've got the measure of it,' said Petros, prodding the fire.

'I wish there was something we could do to help,' said Fyn, once again feeling annoyance towards the agents. He decided it would be safe to tell them more. 'You're right that we're not from around here, and we haven't been here before. What we're doing, well, it's dangerous. We don't want to get anyone in trouble, so if we tell you, you have to promise to keep it secret.'

'You don't need to tell us anything,' said Petros, 'but rest assured we're not about to tell anyone. It's no one else's business after all. As for danger, well we don't need any of that, but if it's anything to go against those morgoons—'

'Petros!' snapped Zara.

'I'll gladly hear it all,' he finished, ignoring her.

'The same for me,' she said, 'and to be truthful it would likely brighten my day.'

Fyn considered his words carefully. 'We're travelling from the north ... and we're not from anywhere around here, but we made friends along the way. They've been captured.'

'It shouldn't have happened,' said Amy. 'We got on the wrong side of the...'

Fyn held his breath as he wondered if she would call them agents...

'...guardians,' she continued after a slight pause, 'and our friends were trying to protect us.'

'That's very unfortunate,' said Petros, 'although it does sound like your friends knew what they were doing. I'm sure you couldn't have changed that.'

'Thanks,' said Fyn, 'but that's why we're here. We're going to get them back.'

Petros coughed and spluttered, nearly choking on thin air.

Zara slapped him enthusiastically on the back.

'Alright! Alright!' he called out. 'Blooming heck! Talk about any excuse to clobber me!' He batted her arm away and looked to Fyn and Amy. 'The two of you? You're going to break into the cells of Atlantis and hope to escape alive?'

'*Atlantis?*' they asked in surprise.

'Of course Atlantis! You want to break into it, and you don't even know what it's called! Oh my days!' He shook his head in disbelief. 'I'd need to sit down if I weren't already!'

The four of them stared into the fire.

'I thought Atlantis was a legend,' said Fyn, thinking of the lost city he had heard stories about, and the way it had supposedly vanished by sinking into the sea many years ago. 'We just thought this was the City of the Sea.'

'It *is* a legend,' said Petros, 'but that doesn't mean it isn't real.'

'And most people *do* call it the City of the Sea,' said Zara, 'but imagine how many cities there are by the sea. They can't all be named the same thing. This one is Atlantis.'

Petros threw a small branch into the fire which crackled loudly in response, spitting out embers. 'The city that supposedly appeared out of nowhere one day, island and all, and has been here ever since. Sounds impossible if you ask me.'

Fyn and Amy looked at each other, both transfixed. Scott had told them the past disaster had transferred entire land masses from one world to another. Could it be that the legendary lost city of Atlantis vanished from their Earth and ended up here? He wondered why Scott hadn't mentioned it but pushed the thought away – his memories from the river were still too raw. So this was the sort of thing that could happen if the agents used his dad to work on world windows. There was no time to waste.

'You must listen to me,' said Petros. 'Trying to get into that place undiscovered is madness. You'll end up in those cells yourselves – or worse.'

'We've got to try,' said Fyn. 'We can't leave them in there. Every moment matters.'

'I can tell you're determined,' Petros replied, 'but tell me you have a plan. Any idea how you're going to do it at all?'

Fyn shuffled his feet.

'We don't have a choice,' said Amy, 'but we will do it, one way or another.'

'Now now, dear,' said Zara. 'No one's judging you.' She glared briefly at Petros before speaking to Amy again. 'You're courageous, I'll give you that, but has it occurred to you that walking into the heart of Atlantis unprepared, risks the very thing your friends tried to protect you from?'

Fyn looked away from her. He knew Mya and Art wouldn't like it. He knew the agents could use him against his dad. 'We just can't get caught,' he said. 'We can't do what we have to do without them.'

'What do you have to do?' asked Zara.

Fyn and Amy remained silent.

Petros sighed. 'You're going to need a little bit more understanding of the place if you want in.'

'You'll help us?' Fyn asked.

'We won't leave you to fend for yourselves,' said Zara. 'There's not much we can do, but we'll get you in as one of us.'

'That's brilliant!' said Fyn. 'Thanks so much!'

'Trojan horse,' said Amy smugly.

He poked his tongue out at her.

'Let's get some food prepared and settle down properly,' said Zara. 'Other travellers will arrive during the night, and we'll want to sort you for the morning before then. We're certainly going to have our work cut out for us...'

CHAPTER TWENTY-SEVEN

The Citadel

'Are you feeling lucky?' Petros asked the next morning as sunlight spread across the sky.

Fyn wasn't sure. 'What if they recognise us?'

'Are they expecting to see you with *us?*' Petros asked.

'I guess not,' said Fyn.

'Then they won't,' said Petros with confidence. 'They don't pay peasant folk much attention at all.'

They ate breakfast and packed up their blankets as the energy field across the archway to the city disappeared and the bridge phased back into place. Agents took up their positions where they'd been the day before, and then it was time to check into the city – Atlantis.

Fyn could still hardly believe it. So much had changed in such a short space of time.

Petros led them, along with Munch – the creature pulling their cart – towards the bridge with a crowd of others. At least thirty groups had arrived overnight, and the path was cluttered with their supplies. The people were lively and chatty but the closer they got to the agents, the less cheerful they became.

Approaching the check in point, Fyn tried to ignore his nerves as he noticed the yellow stripes on the agent's shoulders and wondered about their rank. What if this wasn't such a good idea after all?

He stood with Amy beside Petros and Zara as they reached the agents.

One looked them over and screwed up his eyes. 'You two,' he said to Petros and Zara. 'You're from Farfields?'

'That we are,' replied Petros, scratching beneath his beard.

'I thought so,' said the agent. 'I've seen you before.'

Petros nodded calmly.

Zara smiled but said nothing.

'It's usually just the two of you, isn't it?' the agent asked.

'Very true,' said Petros.

Fyn began to sweat and massaged his fingers into his palms behind his back.

The agent tilted his head towards Fyn and Amy. 'Who are they?' he asked.

'My sister's children,' said Zara. 'She's unwell. We said we'd bring them to keep them out of mischief.'

Fyn and Amy nodded.

'We can be a bit of a handful,' said Amy.

Fyn couldn't believe it.

'Is that true?' the agent asked, looking directly at them.

'Umm. Sometimes,' said Fyn.

The agent stepped aside and spoke quietly with his colleague.

'It will be fine,' Zara whispered to Fyn and Amy.

The agent returned. 'On you go, and make sure to behave yourselves.'

'We will,' said Fyn with his fingers crossed behind his back.

'Not quite as smooth as I'd expected,' Petros mumbled as they walked to the bridge, 'but good enough.'

Fyn rubbed his palms onto his top to dry the sweat from them and looked down at the energy bridge as they crossed it. Despite its glowing blue light, it was transparent, and through it he could see all the way to the waves below. For a moment, he imagined it disappearing beneath his feet – then wobbled and wished he hadn't.

Amy gave a nervous whimper next to him.

'Sorry,' he said, brushing against her arm.

'If I disliked the agents before, I hate them now,' she said so that only he could hear. 'This bridge is torture.'

'You're right,' he agreed, thinking that even though he missed him, he was glad Henry Flame didn't have to deal with it too.

They walked under the archway and into the city, the path they were on leading straight to the citadel. Sprouting off from it, other paths followed the curving city walls round and out of sight behind pearl towers so smooth they looked like they had never been touched, let alone built centuries ago. The energy platforms around them floated in mid-air and, just like the bridge, he could see right through them.

Bright leafy palms lined the streets with pink and blue flowers, and the central path they were on bridged over small streams in brooks which flowed around the city. Turquoise, white, and gold mosaic tiling decorated them with images of marine creatures. Some, like dolphins, turtles, and sharks, he recognised, but there were others which were completely new to him with long necks, wide fins, ginormous tentacles and, of course, pointy teeth.

Just like when they arrived at Homehill, the people were busy going about their business, but unlike the friendly villagers back there, none of the city folk paid them any attention as they walked with their cart to the steps outside the citadel.

'This is where we take the stock,' said Petros. 'There's an offering room inside.'

'We can show you around a little,' said Zara. 'Not that we know our way other than where we're told to go, but it'll give you a chance to explore.'

'Won't they question it when you leave without us?' Amy asked.

'*If* they ask,' said Petros, 'we'll say you're coming back later with others, but I doubt it will be a problem. There are different guardians when you check out.'

'Thank you again,' said Fyn. 'Really.'

'Everything you say screams danger,' he replied, 'and make no mistake I know you may be trouble for us, but I can't help enjoying your madness.' He smiled.

'Don't get any ideas, you,' Zara scolded him. 'We have a home to think about – even if I'd love to see the guardians face some chaos.'

'Guardians and chaos. Definitely up for that!' said Amy cheekily, right as some agents walked by. She quickly turned away, almost making it look like she was hiding something.

The agents stopped and considered her momentarily before losing interest and walking away.

She blushed. 'Sorry! I wasn't thinking.'

'We'd best get this over with,' said Petros, beginning to unload the cart. 'It will take several trips to clear this lot, even with your help.'

They each took a share of the load then joined others climbing the steps to the citadel. The golden dome rose up in front of them, finely engraved with images of stars and constellations.

The main entrance hall had an arched ceiling high above them, intricately painted with depictions of ancient warriors – possibly the true Atlanteans of legend. Lining the hall were emerald-green pillars, rippled with golden leaf and reminding Fyn of sunlight flickering through shallow waves to a sandy seabed. Less pleasing were the agents stationed at each exit from the room.

At the end of the entrance hall, they crossed through another archway into a smaller corridor which led to a junction. An agent directed them to their right, and they followed a small group of people until they reached a large room filled with tables and empty crates. The group ahead of them started to place their supplies into the crates at the back of the room.

'Fruit and vegetables over here,' said Petros, leading them to the side. Then he whispered to Fyn and Amy, 'I'm not sure you'll get the chance now. You'd best come back with us this time.'

They dropped off their supplies and made their way back to the cart at the steps to the citadel.

Fyn observed as much as he could. There had to be a way to do this. His dad depended on it. Mya and Art too.

He considered the outside of the building. *Too exposed*, he thought, as he watched the energy lifts.

At Zara's suggestion, they carried less with them on their second trip in. By spreading the load, they could take more time to investigate.

When they returned to the offering room, Fyn spotted a door at the back. 'What's on the other side of that?'

'No idea,' Zara replied.

Petros shrugged. 'We've never been past here.'

'It's the only door I've seen without guardians,' Fyn said, wondering if it was their way forward.

No one looked thrilled at the idea of trying it, but at least it was something.

'You should go in without us,' he said to Petros and Zara as they returned to the cart again.

They each gave him a puzzled look.

'It's just ... maybe that way they'll be less likely to notice if we don't leave together. We'll meet you back here if we can't get through that door.'

Zara sighed. 'I'm not sure.'

'Me neither,' said Petros, 'although I'm stuck for a better plan.'

Zara gave Fyn and Amy a quick hug each. 'If we don't see you, we'll have to assume you made it. We'll keep watch as we go though, just in case.'

'We'll stop for a while after the first turn on the path outside the city,' said Petros. 'It will give you time to catch up to us or allow us time to hear of any news.'

'Let's get this over with,' said Zara. 'Good luck. Make it count!'

'You're both the best!' said Amy.

'You really are,' said Fyn.

'Just try not to get caught,' urged Petros, 'and we're rooting for you!' he added with a grin.

Then he and Zara made their way up the steps and into the citadel, with only a subtle glance back.

Fyn took his time shifting fruit on the cart. When a small group neared them and started up the steps, he and Amy grabbed some supplies and followed closely behind.

As before, the agent at the junction directed them to their right, but they remained at the back of the group, trying to go unnoticed.

They were careful to avoid eye contact as they passed Petros and Zara on the way to the offering room. Then they took their time putting things in the crates as they waited for a moment alone.

When it arrived, Fyn rushed to the door, drew a deep breath, and pushed on the handle.

It opened to a clear corridor.

'Quick!' he called quietly, eager to get through.

Amy dropped her supplies into the crates and ran to join him. 'I can't believe we're doing this. Totally down the rabbit hole.'

Fyn spotted the excited glint in her eyes as they went through the door.

CHAPTER TWENTY-EIGHT

Freedom Calling

Fyn couldn't help but laugh a little. It was a nervous excitement; the thought of finding his dad after so long both amazed and terrified him. Everything they were doing felt like madness, yet somehow it was working. It had to work. They'd come too far and lost too much to fail.

'What now?' asked Amy? 'Shall we lie low for a while, Dimitry-style?'

'I don't think we can,' he replied. 'If we wait too long then we'll be stuck when the bridge disappears.'

'So you want to dive in?' she asked.

'Not exactly,' he said, trying to think of something helpful. 'I know the Southern Tower didn't really go to plan, but maybe we need a distraction.'

'Yikes,' she replied, 'but I guess that makes sense. Any thoughts on how we'd do that?'

'Not yet,' he confessed, wishing he had a better answer.

They kept close to the walls while moving from one empty corridor to another.

Just as he started to wonder if it was weird that there were no people around, a young man in clothes similar to theirs hurried across the end of the corridor. He was so busy balancing a tray of empty bowls that he didn't see them.

Running as quietly as possible to keep up with him, they poked their heads around the corner just in time to see him disappear down some stairs.

'Hey,' said Fyn in a flash of inspiration. 'We should follow him!'

'What are you thinking?' Amy asked.

'He might be going to a kitchen.'

She frowned. 'It's hardly the time for a snack, Fyn.'

'Come on!' he said, ignoring her and pulling her arm. 'Think of the time Mr Ashley exploded the flask in science class.'

'An amazing day!' she replied.

'He had the Bunsen burner set up and forgot about—'

'—the gas!' she exclaimed.

'Exactly! If he's off to some kitchens, there's got to be something like that we can use for a distraction! Ready?' he asked as they reached the top of the stairs.

In response, Amy ducked against the wall and glanced down the staircase. In full on spy mode, she held up an arm and signalled for him to follow.

Halfway down, the door at the bottom flew open, and a large man with sweat dripping from his bright red face yelled at them. 'What do you think you're doing loitering around? Get down here now!'

They glanced back up the stairs.

'I don't have time for this,' he yelled again. 'Move it, or I'll report you! Are you new or something?'

This was it. Fyn walked down the stairs towards him. 'Sorry, sir,' he said. 'We won't mess up again. We *are* new and not used to it here yet.'

'You better get used to it fast,' said the man, leading them through the door and into an immense kitchen where people were busily preparing food. The young man they'd seen before passed them on his way back out, then rushed up the stairs.

'Things work by you doing as you're told and being where you need to be,' the large man grunted, but his tone had softened a little.

'We really are sorry,' said Fyn, looking around for a way to cause a scene.

'We got lost,' said Amy.

The man glared at them. 'If you mess up you won't be the only ones feeling it. Now come on! I've got a kitchen to run.' He poured a lumpy grey liquid into bowls and held them out on two thin wooden trays.

Fyn held his breath and resisted the urge to gag. It smelt like a cross between fresh cowpats and used gym socks.

'Take these to the units on level three. I trust you know the way!' He passed them a tray each but must have seen their confusion because he tutted. 'Up out of here. Two lefts to the main stairway. When you get to level three take a right and follow the corridor.'

'Thanks,' said Fyn.

'Don't thank me. Get it done right and maybe *I'll* thank *you!*'

They smiled at him innocently.

'Come on – move! You kids don't know what's good for you,' he muttered as he started chopping fruit.

'Err,' said Fyn, as an idea occurred to him.

'What?' asked the man, turning red in the face again.

'Is it true...' Fyn began, '...that there are *prisoners* in this place?'

The man glowered at them.

'It's just,' said Amy, cottoning on, 'I think they must be awfully scary.'

Fyn nodded. 'I'd hate to go near them...'

The man blinked back at them. 'You're telling me you're nervous of prisoners?'

Fyn nodded again.

'You might have the wrong job then!' He laughed. 'Don't worry this time. The prisoners are on level five. Now go!'

They left the kitchen and went back up the stairs.

Fyn wore a smug grin on his face.

'That was *so* close!' said Amy.

'I know,' he replied, 'but at least we know the way, even though we'll be more visible than ever.'

'Chameleons hide in plain sight,' she replied in her most knowing voice. 'We just have to act as though we're doing our jobs. Agents don't pay attention to peasant folk. That's what Petros said.'

They took the first left and Fyn shivered. Something felt different, but he didn't know why. It was almost as though something was tugging at a long-lost memory.

There was only one room partway along the corridor, and it was blocked by the twisting silver bars of gates in the shape of a large and magnificent trident.

He looked through into the room beyond. The walls were golden, and the ceiling domed. In the centre of the room was some kind of pedestal. He didn't know why, but he was drawn to it.

'Fyn, come on!' Amy nudged his arm.

He nearly dropped his tray but reluctantly continued.

They took the next left and reached the main stairway which spiralled up far above them, its ivory banister covered in tiny, smooth shells.

The first few floors were busy but, cautiously, they passed the third floor and no one paid them any attention. By the time they reached the fifth floor, no one else was in sight.

'That would have been much nicer with an indoor lift!' Amy complained as they stepped off the staircase.

Fyn faltered, realising he might be about to see his dad for the first time in eight years. All that time wondering where he was and longing to see him. All that worrying if he had somehow driven him away, of questioning if he had done anything wrong. It had led to this moment.

'Eromlos to Fyn,' said Amy. 'You need to snap out of it.' She had put her tray down and was taking his from him. She looked him in the eyes. 'Don't worry. He'll be everything you want and more. I'm here as much as you need me to be.'

'Thanks,' he mumbled in a daze.

'This isn't the time to go all dreamer on me though,' she said. 'People are counting on us, whether they know it or not.'

'Sorry,' he said, pulling himself together. He knew she was right.

'Don't be sorry – be practical.' She cringed. 'Bleurgh! I sounded like my mum then! Ready?'

'Ready,' he replied, and to his surprise, he was.

Chapter Twenty-Nine

Rescue

Carrying their trays of stinky grey stodge, Fyn and Amy continued along the landing and turned to their right.

'Follow my lead,' said Amy.

They walked down a particularly long corridor until they reached two agents at the entrance to the cells – a man with his arms folded behind his head, and a woman leaning her head on her hands. Both appeared to be extremely bored.

Amy strolled straight up to them. 'Sorry to disturb you,' she started, 'but one of you is wanted in the offering room. Apparently, things have got out of hand. We were asked to send someone down. They'll need a cell prepared,' she added.

Despite the fact that he was completely confused, Fyn nodded vigorously.

'I'll go,' the man replied, jumping keenly to his feet and leaving the woman with a frown on her face as he disappeared towards the stairs.

'What are you waiting for?' she asked them. 'Don't you have food to deliver?'

'I'm sorry,' said Amy. 'I'm... not feeling... *Argh!*'. She dropped her tray and fell to the floor.

'Amy!' Fyn moved to help, getting between her and the agent, but Amy glared at him and mouthed for him to 'back off.'

The agent stepped closer. 'Look at that mess! What's the matter with you?'

Fyn looked at the broken bowls and grey slop spread across the floor, then to Amy who was pointedly looking back and forth between him and the agent. Surely, she didn't want...

'Oh, for goodness' sake!' said Amy. Then she swung her leg out and swept it underneath the agent's legs, knocking her to the floor. Next, she grabbed her food tray and hit the agent over the head with it.

'Amy!' said Fyn, completely bewildered. 'What are you doing?'

She had already leapt on to the woman's back and was trying to pin her to the ground.

'She's not our friend, Fyn! Quick! Get the vine out of my sling!'

He did as he was told, throwing his tray to the side and dashing to help.

Sitting on the agent's legs, he tied her ankles together and her arms behind her back. Then, unceremoniously, he pulled a piece of cloth from his own sling and apologised as he shoved it into the agent's mouth.

'Eww, Fyn! Really?'

'It's clean ... ish!' he said, considering the jungle, the river, and the pool. 'Besides...' he gestured at Amy and the agent as he stood up. 'Where did all *that* come from?'

'Oh, I don't know,' she shrugged. 'Just something I saw on television. I've always wanted to try it, and she'll be fine. It's a risk of her job! Anyway, let's hurry! We won't have long before the other one comes back.'

They sped along the corridor, looking through the red energy fields at the entrances to each of the cells. So far, they were empty.

'Why didn't you send her off with the other one?' Fyn asked as they checked.

Amy shrugged. 'I thought it might be helpful to keep someone around.'

'Over here!' came a voice. 'I wondered what the noise was!'

They rushed over to find Art in a cell.

'What are you doing here?' Art asked, but his tired eyes looked relieved.

'It's obvious, isn't it?' Fyn replied with a grin. 'We're breaking you out!'

'We thought you'd go back and get help,' said Mya in the cell next to Art.

'You can thank us later,' said Amy, 'but right now we need you. How can we get you out of here?'

'And my dad...' started Fyn.

'He's not here,' said Mya.

It was like he walked into a wall. He felt the air leave his lungs and his legs turn to jelly as disappointment washed over him. It was in Amy's face too. She looked breathless – momentarily stunned.

'We can't stop now,' she said, recovering first. 'We have to keep going!' Her hands were on his shoulders. She stared him in the face. 'Are you with me?'

He nodded half-heartedly but felt like he was sinking. Did this mean his dad wasn't there at all? Perhaps the agents had him in a lab and were progressing with their plans.

Amy turned back to Mya and Art. 'How do we get you out?' she asked again.

'The panel by the agent,' said Art. 'It's what they use.'

Amy ran to it, leaping over the agent wriggling on the floor.

Fyn followed but felt like he wasn't there. How could they have travelled so far and still not found his dad? How could he be missing again?

'We'll find him, Fyn!' he heard Amy telling him, but he was so frustrated. *How could this have happened?* He looked at the panel. Remembering the way they moved the soarer back at the Southern Tower, he held his hand against it, but it didn't react.

Amy called to Mya and Art. 'It's not working!'

Impatiently, Fyn picked up his tray from the floor and rammed the corner of it into the panel.

'Fyn,' said Amy, 'you don't need to do that...'

He didn't listen.

He took all his annoyance, all his disappointment, and even his exhaustion and smashed the tray hard into the panel again and again, ignoring the tears forming behind his eyes.

The tray split down the middle.

'It's working!' said Amy. 'The fields – they did a sort of flicker!'

He threw the tray to the floor where it broke in half. Then he picked up the other one and hit the panel again.

The panel cracked.

He watched as the energy fields sealing the cells flickered again and vanished. Then, his arms sore, he dropped the tray.

'Fyn are you...?'

'I'm fine,' he replied, harsher than intended, but there was no time to apologise as the lights cut out.

For a moment, he had no idea what was happening. Then the ceiling lit up, completely covered by a bright purple block of pulsing energy.

'Run!' shouted Mya, racing out with Art to meet them as the energy began to descend from the ceiling.

Fyn looked up, brought back to his senses. The purple light was burning the walls – burning everything in its path.

A stranger with scruffy black hair ran from another cell and dashed past them all. As he did, he shouted over his shoulder, 'I'd do what she says!'

The burning light moved ever closer.

'Come on!' shouted Amy, but Fyn saw the panic-stricken eyes of the agent squirming on the floor.

'Help me with her!' he urged.

Art bent down and scooped her up with one arm. Then they ran as the light gained on them, Art ducking as it nearly touched his head.

Fyn realised why the corridor was so long. It was a defence mechanism. He ducked with the others. The staircase was in sight.

Practically crawling at pace, Art threw himself and the agent forward, screaming out as the light burned his back. He made it.

Fyn and the others sped through as fast as they could, collapsing on the floor as the purple light reached the ground behind them and disappeared.

'Never again … but thank you,' said Mya, closing her eyes and shaking her head in disbelief.

Art's face was screwed up in pain. On his back, his skin showed through a hole burned into his top. It was bright red, weeping, and blotchy.

'We'll need to see to that soon,' said Mya. 'Are you okay to keep moving?'

He grimaced. 'I'll be fine.'

'We need to go,' said Fyn. 'We have to work out what to do next.'

'What about your dad?' asked Amy.

'I'm not giving up on him,' he replied, 'but we can't help him if we're captured.'

'Which way?' asked Art.

Fyn tried to think. Maybe they could still come out the way they came in, through the offering hall with the other travellers. 'Follow me.'

Leaving the agent behind, he led them down the stairway, turning at the bottom into the corridor with the silver gates. As he passed them, he stopped. The gates were ajar.

He couldn't explain it but, somehow, he knew. 'I need to go in here.'

'Are you crazy?' Amy asked, clearly not trying to hide her surprise.

'Maybe,' he replied. 'Come if you want, or stay here, or go. I'll catch up if I have to, but I've got to do this.'

He pushed one of the gates and it swung steadily inwards, opening into the large domed room. He could hear Mya and Art arguing in hushed voices with Amy behind him, but for some reason he didn't care. He walked in.

The golden walls were decorated with inscription like at the towering stones and the ancient ruins. A language he didn't understand. *What does it mean?* he wondered. *What is this place?*

He reached the centre of the room. What he'd previously thought of as a pedestal was something else. There was a large circular platform in the middle of it and a small blank panel on the front, like the ones on the soarers and the one from the cells.

The others had stopped arguing and followed him in.

'Fyn,' said Mya. 'We have to go before it's too late. We can't be here.'

He hardly heard her. He looked at his outstretched hand and, lowering it slowly in front of him, placed his palm on the panel.

A blast of energy charged through him.

Crying out in shock and pain he attempted to pull his hand away, but the energy held him still. His body pulsed as he felt himself being lifted high above the ground. His arms and legs were stretched out, away from his centre.

He tried to move but was stuck in mid-air. He began to feel hot – too hot – like he was burning from the inside.

His skin started to glow and, unable to control himself, he screamed in agony.

Amy and the others called out, trying to approach him, but it was no use. He could see the fear in their eyes as an invisible force held them back.

'What can we do?' Amy shouted, but whatever held Fyn began to lower him.

He felt his feet touch the ground as the glow wore away, and he was returned to his previous position with his palm flat against the panel. The pain was nearly gone. All he could think about was how badly he wanted his family.

The others rushed to his side, and from the edges of the room, neon-blue energy forked its way across the floor in channels that led to the platform.

He watched, transfixed, as it spiralled up and around to the central circle. Then a projection of bright light burst from it, and the light was shaped like a man.

His dad.

Chapter Thirty

Betrayal

Fyn stared in disbelief at the image of his dad projected in front of them. It looked just like the man he remembered, although tired and a little older. He couldn't think. He didn't have the faintest idea how to react. So much was happening. Then the projection spoke.

'Where to begin… I shouldn't be here. I should be with my family.'

It hit Fyn hard.

'Dad?' he asked reluctantly, but he knew it was just a recording. The voice brought back so much feeling. He had tried to recall it so many times but after so long it didn't always come easily. *This* he knew. Like the image, the memories it brought back were vivid. He could trust it. A tear rolled down his cheek.

'If I'm right and this message is played,' the projection continued, 'I can only believe it will be to you, Fyn. I'm so sorry I wasn't there for you. Then and now. I've never lost hope in getting back to you and your mother. I've always planned to somehow, but as the years have passed it has sometimes felt less likely. It seems like only yesterday I was tucking you into bed, telling you stories. I hope you remember those times. I treasure them.'

The image of Daniel Carter sighed.

'Anyway... I sort of pray you'll never hear this message because, if you do, danger won't be far behind.'

Fyn didn't want to take his eyes off the projection, but he had to glance back at the others, if only to believe this was happening – to be certain it wasn't his imagination. The shocked expressions on their faces were reassuring. It was just as unexpected to them as to him. He looked back at the projection as his dad continued speaking.

'I've been in this world for ... too long, although there are good people here. I have friends, but it's a complicated place and things are not as simple as they appear to be. A few months ago, I started noticing inconsistencies; small things weren't adding up. I did some digging and didn't like what I found. I should have acted the same a little longer. Maybe things would have been different if I hadn't shown signs of change, but I had to do something ... or at least try. You and I, Fyn, we're connected to more than we knew.'

Fyn was so intrigued. *Connected to what?* What was he talking about?

'I came here to the Hall of Records,' the projection of his dad continued, 'seeking a way to get back to you. I discovered a record which would only work for us, locked so no one else could open it. I erased it so it can never be heard by the wrong ears, but if you ever find yourself in this place, I sense it will be life-changing. I've done all I can for now, so I must go into hiding.'

Fyn moved closer to the projection, almost willing him not to go.

'Don't trust the guardians,' his dad said clearly, 'and, as much as I hate to say it, if you meet my old friend Scott – don't trust him either. He's working with them and threatened me, trying to make me join them. That's why I had to move on, but I'm scared they'll try and come for you to get to me. You're more important than you can possibly imagine. This city – it's part of our history. I think we might be ... descendants. I know I'm a scientist, but what's happening is more than I can explain. It's like destiny, and I believe you're the one who will find a safe and stable way, Fyn. You will be our way between worlds.'

Goosebumps spread across Fyn's body from head to toe.

'I truly am sorry I haven't been there all these years,' the projection continued. 'I hope I'll see you again someday. If you're hearing this, I'm sure I will. There are bigger things

241

at play now. If he's still around, look out for your Grandad Bernie, and always take care of your mum. I love you, Fyn.'

The projection faded and Fyn wanted to reach out and grab it, holding on to his dad forever, but the neon-blue energy had already retracted from the platform and was now working its way across the floor to the edges of the room where it disappeared.

'That makes *that* clear,' said a cold voice from behind them.

Fyn and the others span around to find themselves face to face with several agents: four with purple stripes on their shoulders, and another – the one who had spoken – with silver stripes on his. Next to him, and looking perfectly healthy, was Scott.

Fyn staggered backwards, drawing a sharp breath.

'There's a reason he fled,' the agent continued to Scott, each of his words like a spit of deadly venom. 'You were too obvious.' He cast his gaze at Fyn and the others. 'All of you stay where you are.'

Scott's face was expressionless.

The agents who hadn't spoken directed their blasters at them all, moving in perfect unison.

'Scott...' His name caught in Mya's throat. 'We thought you'd... How...? Why are you with them?'

'Because he *is* with us, idiot,' said the silver-striped agent. His face was gaunt and his eyes narrow.

'Aris,' Scott warned.

'I don't understand,' said Fyn. 'I trusted you.'

It was Aris who replied. 'Shut up, boy. Listening to you makes it clear why your waste of a father didn't try harder to get home.'

'That's enough!' said Scott, the authority in his voice evident. A flash of rage crossed his face, but his expression soon became blank again.

The man named Aris looked at him with resentment. 'Fine! Do what you must, but don't waste more time!'

'We needed you,' Scott said directly to Fyn. 'That's the reason we brought you here. Your father was careless. He was overheard at the end of recording the message you've just listened to. Although we were unable to play it back ourselves, thanks to him, we knew it was for you.'

'What does that have to do with anything?' asked Fyn.

'You must know by now that panels read energy. With your message locked and him in hiding, we sought you instead.'

'But why work with them in the first place?' Fyn asked. He couldn't understand why his dad's best friend would do this.

'You're a fool,' sneered Aris.

'Be quiet,' said Scott firmly, and Aris backed down again.

'Your father was my closest friend. He always has been, but he didn't see the way things are.'

'And how *are* they?' Fyn asked, irritation beginning to seep through him.

'We can't stop the agents. We need to be on their side. With the technology they command, we might be able to find a better way together.'

'You know you can't trust them!' urged Mya. 'They have no honour! Why has yours abandoned you?'

Scott closed his eyes, but instead of retaliating as Fyn had expected, he spoke calmly to him. 'I tried to work with your father, but he didn't feel the same as me.'

'Is that why you turned on him?' Fyn asked, his voice slightly raised.

'Traitor!' hissed Mya.

One of the agents directed their blaster at her throat.

'Put that down,' Scott ordered.

The agent obeyed immediately.

How could this be the same person Fyn had trusted? The person he thought had been helping him? 'Who *are* you?' he asked.

Scott shrugged. 'It takes all sorts to make a world.'

Fyn remembered the way those words had given him so much hope back in Grandad Bernie's kitchen and felt a hatred towards them. How could Scott act this way and yet stand there so calmly? What kind of person had he become? 'What would Marina think of you?' he asked scathingly.

'Don't pretend you know what you're talking about!' Scott fired up, showing real emotion at last. 'You get to play the hurt child but have no idea what's happening in this world. It's time to grow up!'

'Don't talk to him like that!' shouted Amy, her hands rolled into fists.

'Don't make me quieten you,' Scott replied.

She looked him straight in the eyes. 'I'd like to see you try.'

Fyn was keen to move the conversation on. 'How did you survive the blast and the river?'

'I was only stunned,' said Scott. 'After they fished me out of the rapids, they brought me here. Then I spoke to the right people and confirmed I work with them – not all of them know I do. It was less than ideal, but I hoped losing me might make you more determined to rescue your father.'

'As if I don't already want to find him!'

'There's more to it than that. I could have easily forced your hand, but it wouldn't have worked. You needed to believe you could get here, and to do it by choice.'

'Why?' Fyn asked.

'The panel behind you. It's like how you controlled the soarer back at the Southern Tower. You had to want to move it. The message here wouldn't have played if you were conflicted. It's about your energy. We couldn't have forced that.'

Fyn understood. The moment before the projection had appeared, he had longed for his family. He thought back to the panel at the cells. Even if he hadn't been conflicted it wouldn't have worked. It had been locked to the prison guards. Why then had he been able to move the soarer at the Southern Tower? *They probably weren't locked*, he realised. *No one would be crazy enough to take one in this world.*

'We led you here,' said Scott. 'We made sure it was the only place you could ultimately reach because we needed you, and more than that, we needed you to *want* to be here.'

Bewildered, Fyn shook his head. 'You did all of this to hear one message? How much of it did you even hear?'

'Enough to know you're important,' said Scott.

'You realise we all nearly died at the cells?' Mya asked.

'That wasn't part of the plan,' Scott replied. 'For what it's worth, I'm glad you didn't.'

She frowned and looked away from him.

'When I walked past this room,' said Fyn, deciding to voice another concern. 'I felt something. What was that?'

'I've no idea,' said Scott. 'We only opened the gates.'

'And what the panel did to me?'

Scott looked clueless. 'What do you mean?'

Fyn didn't answer. He wasn't about to tell him if he hadn't seen it happen.

'After the Southern Tower,' Art said unexpectedly, 'Florentina told us she as good as heard confirmation Daniel was here.'

'She said the agents spoke of a man from Rogan's village,' Scott replied. '*If* they meant Daniel, it's still true. He was here. He just didn't stay.'

'What if they *didn't* mean Daniel?' Fyn asked. 'Oh,' he said, scowling as he realised they could have meant Scott.

Scott shrugged. 'Whatever she meant, I let it work in my favour. It helped me to bring you here.'

'I can't believe that I trusted you,' said Fyn. 'Even that crazy man with his dog told me not to.'

'Martin was an idiot,' Scott replied. 'Twisted and jealous. His orders were to gain your trust and encourage you to join me, but he tried to prevent it. He spent years as an agent on Earth, hoping to one day travel between worlds himself. When a young boy like you was allowed the privilege before him he despised it. Ironically, his plan drove you here anyway. It was exactly what I wanted but not what I'd expected. I'd banked on you coming alone, and not so soon. I was unprepared.'

'You needed to return to Homehill first,' explained Art.

Scott nodded. 'I couldn't raise suspicion at home by suddenly disappearing. Listen, Art. As your friend, it's easier for you all to do as you're told right now.'

'The agents came that night,' said Fyn, ignoring Scott's plea and the way he was trying to reason with them. 'They flew right over us. Why didn't you signal them?'

'For the same reason they attacked at the river. They don't all know I'm working with them. I couldn't risk things escalating and them taking us in. Don't forget you had to want to be here.'

'Enough!' demanded Aris. 'We have work to do!'

'They deserve the truth,' said Scott. 'There's no harm in it.'

'When you first contacted me,' said Fyn as a sudden thought occurred to him, 'you were in a cave. Something roared in the background before you had to go. You were by the city.'

'Yes,' replied Scott. 'I'd been here and was travelling back to Homehill. The cave seemed a good place to contact you, but I had a close call with something there.'

'Sally...' whispered Amy.

'Now, as Aris has pressed,' said Scott, 'we have some important matters to discuss. We need to understand more about what your father said – about your destiny.'

'Wait,' said Fyn. 'Please, just two more things?'

'Go on,' said Scott.

'Why did you warn me about the agents when you first contacted me? You could have told me they were good and led me to trust them...'

'He has a point,' said Aris, sneering at Scott.

'If you're anything like your father,' Scott replied, 'which I now know you are, your heart would have steadied you against the agents on your own. I wanted you on my side so stuck to the way things are. I hoped giving you some truth would create trust.'

'Thank you,' said Fyn thoughtfully.

'...and the second question?' asked Scott.

Fyn tried to place as much feeling into his next words as possible. 'That's something I don't understand at all,' he said. 'When exactly did you become such a morgoon? Your family would be ashamed.'

Scott's face flushed red.

Amy looked thrilled.

'Take them!' Scott ordered.

CHAPTER THIRTY-ONE

Escape from the City

As the agents moved towards Fyn and the others, multiple laser blasts fired from the gates at the room's entrance. All four agents and Aris fell unconscious to the floor. Scott alone remained standing with the others.

The prisoner Fyn had inadvertently freed back at the cells strode into the room. 'I thought you might need assistance,' he said, throwing one of several blasters he was carrying to Fyn who caught it and held it uncertainly.

'I visited the armoury to make things easier,' the prisoner continued before pointing at Scott. 'Is he one of the good guys? I didn't shoot him because he's dressed like you. Now I'm not so sure.'

'He's not one of us,' said Mya, taking the blaster from Fyn and shooting Scott to the ground.

'Mya!' shouted Art.

'He survived it once. He can do it again,' she replied. 'Oh, and it's set to stun.'

Art shook his head, but the prisoner looked impressed.

'You didn't think I'd give the boy a fully set weapon?'

'Thanks,' said Fyn, unsure what to make of him, 'but we need to get out of here.'

'He's right,' said Amy. 'We can't get caught.'

'Where are you headed?' the prisoner asked.

'Away from the city,' said Fyn. 'Back to the bridge. I don't know any other way.'

'Follow me,' he replied, giving the others spare blasters before turning and leaving the room.

Fyn looked back uncertainly at Scott.

'He made his choice,' said Amy, grabbing Fyn by the arm. 'If we don't leave now, we might not be able to.'

'Shouldn't we go in this direction?' Fyn asked, indicating the way back to the offering room.

'Definitely not,' said the prisoner. 'There'll be far more guardians there.'

'And you have a plan?' asked Mya.

'I do,' he replied, with a grin.

She frowned but the corners of her mouth twitched.

They followed him to what Fyn guessed was the back of the citadel, watching as he stopped two agents with rapid stun blasts.

'Don't we get to know your name?' Amy asked.

'Ezio,' he replied, looking out to some gardens through a window. He hopped up onto the windowsill and dropped a few feet to the grass on the other side. After checking carefully in all directions, he called for them to follow.

They ran through the gardens to the surrounding wall and, one at a time, helped each other climb up and over into an empty street.

'There are nine circles of the city before the bridge,' Ezio explained. 'Keep with me. Hopefully we'll make it before they realise we've left. Try to act like you're meant to be here.'

It was easier said than done. Away from the main path to the citadel they were completely out of place, and the city folk were not shy about staring distrustfully.

Ezio stuck to clearer paths as much as possible, but their time was up.

Sirens blared loudly across the city, screeching out and echoing from building to building. The people around them let out screams of fright, running for cover.

'Come on!' Ezio called, breaking into a sprint when they reached the main path.

Agents rushed out from the entrance to the citadel, and soarers rose into the sky. Anyone delivering supplies stopped in their tracks, but no one paid them any attention as they pleaded their innocence.

'We'll never make it!' shouted Amy, looking to the archway.

'Keep running!' Fyn called back, but it was too late. He watched as the agents reached the bridge and shut it down. The blue energy platform vanished, along with their chances of escape.

People began to huddle as the sirens continued to wail. Agents from the citadel were getting closer and soarers were preparing to settle next to them. More soarers from the other side of the bridge landed nearby, and a large one flew over the city walls before resting next to the archway.

Fyn, Amy, and Mya faced the agents from the citadel. Art and Ezio covered them from behind, opposite the large soarer and the agents by the wall.

They held their blasters steady but were surrounded.

'How are we going to get out of this?' Amy asked.

'I don't know,' Fyn replied, feeling his hope fading.

Scott and Aris stepped out from one of the soarers in front of him.

'Tell them to lower their weapons,' Scott demanded. 'Aris. Do it!'

'As he said,' Aris instructed the agents.

It seemed Scott had been telling the truth. The agents did as commanded but looked confused at the way Aris took an order.

Scott approached Fyn and the others. 'There's nowhere to go. You all know it's true. There's no point in resisting any more.'

'Except to show we're not supporting you!' said Mya.

Scott rubbed his chest where she had blasted him. 'It will only cause harm,' he said. 'Believe it or not, I don't want that.'

'I'm not going anywhere with you,' said Fyn. 'I don't even want to look at you.'

'I can help you find your father,' said Scott. 'I know it feels like I'm the bad guy but, if you work with me, we can make things right.'

Doubt spilled into Fyn's mind. Scott had been his dad's best friend. They had been as close to each other as Fyn and Amy were now. What if things had just got out of hand? What if he really could help? Unlike Aris, he had certainly tried to reason with them.

Reaching out to Fyn, Scott took a step forward.

Fyn hesitated. He had been through so much. What if things could be easier? Was there a way for them to work together? Then he remembered his dad's words, *Don't trust the guardians and, as much as I hate to say it, if you meet my old friend Scott – don't trust him either*. He thought about what Scott had said only a short time ago, *If you're anything like your father, which I now know you are…*

Fyn stepped back.

'Trust me,' Scott urged.

'You need me,' Fyn replied, realising the truth. 'That's what this is about. You needed my dad, and now you need me, but I won't help you. I can't trust you. I never should have.' He took another step back.

'This is a waste of time,' snapped Aris. 'Guardians, take aim!'

'No!' shouted Scott.

Without warning, an agent fell from the large soarer by the archway and landed awkwardly on the ground. He recovered fast and, upon spotting Aris, shouted wildly for everyone to take cover.

Before his words could register, a pulse of clear energy, visible only like a heat wave, came from the soarer he'd fallen from. It spread through them all in a fraction of a second.

'Attack!' screamed Aris, but none of the agent's weapons worked.

In his confusion, Fyn tried his own blaster, directing it at the ground by Aris' feet. It was as useless as everyone else's.

'What are you waiting for?' called a familiar voice, and Fyn felt overjoyed as he saw Grandad Bernie poke his head out from the soarer and his foot kick the agent back to the ground.

'Come on! I'm not supposed to be parked here!'

Fyn ran with the others at the soarer, but Scott and the agents chased.

Scott grabbed Fyn by the wrist. 'It doesn't have to be this way!'

Caught up in the moment, the others around them stopped.

Fyn tried to free himself. 'Let go! This is your fault. You betrayed your best friend! Now you want to betray his son?'

Scott opened his mouth, but no words came out. Instead, his grip loosened ever so slightly, and Fyn pulled free from his grasp.

Aris roared in frustration, but Grandad Bernie shot a blast from the soarer to the ground.

'Oops!' his voice echoed out across the crowd. 'I'd step back if I were you.'

Seizing their chance, Fyn and the others boarded the vehicle.

As soon as he saw Grandad Bernie, Fyn threw his arms around him.

With one hand resting on the soarer's panel, Grandad Bernie did his best to hug him back. 'I'm glad to see you too, short stuff,' he said, the warmth in his voice ringing true. 'Now we have to hurry. Daniel?'

'Not here,' said Fyn.

Grandad Bernie sighed. 'Scott?'

'Not who we thought he was,' said Amy, from behind them.

Grandad Bernie gave them a puzzled look but didn't press further. 'Right then, everyone, hold tight!' With that, he flew the soarer high into the sky and over the city walls.

'You're definitely okay?' Fyn asked Grandad Bernie after checking nobody was following.

'I am,' he replied, 'and you?'

Fyn didn't know where to begin.

'We'll talk soon,' said Grandad Bernie.

'How did you stop the soarers and all those weapons?' Amy asked.

'I used an electromagnetic pulse to disable them ... or something like that,' Grandad Bernie replied casually. 'I'm sure it won't keep them for long.'

'An EMP,' said Amy as she looked away from the doors and windows. 'I'm so impressed right now! Is there ... err ... any way you can level this thing out?' She closed her eyes briefly and held her stomach.

'I'll try,' he replied, 'but there's something back there you might want to focus on in the meantime.' He waved his arm to the rear of the soarer.

Fyn allowed his eyes to follow and, as they adjusted to the dimmed light, a broad smile spread across his face. Henry Flame was peering curiously at them all, poking his head out from under a small blanket.

CHAPTER THIRTY-TWO

Things to Come

Henry Flame moved swiftly from one person to another, greeting them by way of a sniff, as Grandad Bernie flew the soarer above the great path leading into the city and navigated them away from Atlantis.

'Look!' Fyn said to Amy, pointing excitedly below.

Petros and Zara were waiting with Munch and their cart as they'd planned.

'They made it out!' He waved, hoping they would see, as Grandad Bernie swerved the soarer in the direction of the coast.

They spotted Fyn, and he beamed as they jumped up and down with excitement.

Grandad Bernie kept the soarer as low to the treetops as possible. 'Hopefully agents won't follow if they think we went the other way. We just need to turn this thing off before they trace it.'

Fyn felt relieved, and more so as they reached the edge of the jungle and flew above the sandy beach below. Seeing the tide hit the shore was wonderful, but nothing compared to the feeling of being back with his grandad. He had hope again and couldn't wait to catch up and tell him everything.

Mya and Art were opposite Fyn – Mya rubbing herby paste into the wound on Art's back while Art switched off the blasters they'd collected. Ezio was closer to the front, sitting behind Grandad Bernie with his eyes closed.

Who is he, and why was he in the cells? Fyn knew they wouldn't have escaped without him, but he didn't like not knowing why he had been there. Had he committed a crime, or was he another victim of the agents? *Perhaps Mya or Art know*, he considered.

Amy moved to the back of the soarer where she sat cross-legged, twisting her hair around her fingers in a world of her own.

He made a mental note to check on her when they had a moment away from the others.

'This will do,' said Grandad Bernie, steering the soarer between a gap in the cliffs and landing it gently before powering it down. 'We should be okay for a while. Fyn, Amy, will you join me outside?'

After lowering themselves to the ground, Fyn took off his shoes and felt the warm grains of sand spread between his toes.

Grandad Bernie hugged them each tightly. 'I'm so relieved you're okay.'

'Thanks to you,' said Fyn gratefully. 'How did you get here? How did you get a soarer?' He couldn't hide his amazement.

Grandad Bernie chuckled as they started to walk. 'Pretty spectacular, isn't it? I had to trust you were in safe hands after you left Homehill, and I knew others followed you to help, but as each day passed I grew more unsettled. The villagers tried to entertain me, but I made my mind up when Theo and Kali returned with Henry Flame. They told us all about the Southern Tower and that the five of you continued on to the City of the Sea—'

'—Atlantis!' interrupted Fyn, before considering his dad's suggestion that they were related to the city. *How could that be possible?*

Grandad Bernie looked astonished. 'Well, I'll be … but yes, I mean, with everything else I guess I can believe it. After the others told us where you were headed and that Daniel was there, I set off to find you.'

'On your own?' Fyn asked, distracted again by his grandad's story.

'I had Mr Flame with me. Anyway, that's the way I wanted it. I'd learned more about the goings on of this place by then. This morning we came across the soarer back there. Two agents were using it but had stopped for a break. One I left behind with no equipment, and the other … we left him in Atlantis.' He winked.

'Amazing,' said Amy.

Fyn smiled again. 'Best grandad ever. How did you know about the EMP? I mean, the electromagnetic pulse?'

'Let's just say, the agent with me wasn't worried about sharing secrets when he was on his own. Apparently, when the agents started to limit the use of technology on Eromlos, they used EMPs against people. I doubt they've had them used against themselves! I expect they'll change things now!' He chuckled again.

They reached the edge of the gap in the cliffs where they sat with their backs against the rock and faced the sea.

Fyn breathed in the fresh air, enjoying the sun on his skin – until he remembered the way it had glowed back in the Hall of Records.

'That's enough about me,' said Grandad Bernie. 'Tell me about your journey. Who is the man with you, and what happened to Scott?'

He listened attentively as they filled him in on their adventures, never interrupting, except for mini reactions along the way and an accidental curse word when Fyn told him how Scott had betrayed them. Otherwise, he was completely silent at every mention of the projection and the way the energy surge had pulsed through Fyn. When they finished speaking, he admitted he had no idea what Fyn's dad had meant about them being connected to more. 'He said you and he could be descendants of Atlantis?'

Fyn and Amy nodded, but Fyn didn't really know how to process everything that had happened and everything still to come.

'And you're supposed to be the one to find us a safe way of travelling between worlds?' Grandad Bernie asked Fyn.

'That's what Dad said,' he replied, *but I have no idea how*, he thought.

'We'll find a way,' said Grandad Bernie, as though reading his mind. 'It's like I said in the garden when you arrived at my house – it seems there *is* a bigger picture connecting the dots somehow.'

They walked back to the soarer.

Mya was watching Art as he waved an old stick to and fro. Henry Flame chased it happily until he saw Grandad Bernie. Then he ran excitedly to him, looping around Fyn and Amy on the way.

Fyn surprised himself as a laugh escaped his lips. 'He seems to be doing okay!'

Grandad Bernie smiled. 'I'd say he's as good as normal again now.'

Ezio swung his legs from the edge of the soarer, hopping down and wiping his hair from his eyes as they approached.

'I believe some thanks are in order,' said Grandad Bernie.

Ezio smiled. 'Without you, we'd be back in the cells by now, so *I* thank you – and also *you*,' he added to Fyn and Amy, 'for freeing me in the first place.'

He reached forward and shook their hands.

'You're most welcome,' said Grandad Bernie as Art and Mya settled next to them. 'I've been brought up to speed on most events, and I cannot express enough how grateful I am to you all for keeping these two as safe as possible. That said,' he added to Ezio, 'if you are to come with us, I must ask why you were imprisoned.'

'I understand,' he replied, 'but I'm not quite ready to share every detail. I hope it's enough to say I was protecting my sister, and the guardians took it personally. I've been in the cells ever since. If you'll have me, I'll help as I can. You can lose me whenever you like.'

Fyn noted the use of the word "guardians". If he came with them, they might have some explaining to do.

'Good enough for me,' said Grandad Bernie. 'Everyone else?'

They all agreed.

'Okay,' he said. 'Now we have a plan to sort.'

'Where do we start?' asked Fyn.

'Back at the village I think,' Grandad Bernie replied.

Mya shook her head. 'They'll expect us to go there.'

'We'll have to eventually,' said Fyn, thinking of his dad's paperwork. 'There might be answers there somewhere.'

'Plus, we need to tell them about Scott,' said Amy.

'Is everything alright?' Fyn mouthed to her as the others continued talking.

'I think so,' she replied quietly. 'I'll be better when we get home. Big things ahead for you.' She smiled as she nudged him. 'I'm okay.'

He hoped it was true.

'You know none of you need to come with us,' Grandad Bernie said to Mya, Art, and Ezio. 'We'll gladly accept your company, but it's bound to be dangerous as we keep searching for Daniel.'

'I'll stay,' said Mya. 'He's as much one of us, as one of you.'

'And I think you'll need all the help you can get,' said Art. 'There's a lot more to this place than you've seen so far.'

Ezio looked at him curiously. 'I know nothing of Daniel, but I'd say we'll be better together than apart.' He looked to Grandad Bernie. 'I owe you.'

Fyn took it all in as Henry Flame settled comfortably by his side. He knew the adventure was only just beginning, but somehow, he felt okay. He could finally trust that his dad loved him, and he had faith at last in knowing he hadn't been abandoned. Looking around at Grandad Bernie, Amy,

Henry Flame, and the others, he was grateful not to be alone as he realised he never had been.

Stretching out his fingers, he pondered for a tiny moment as they tingled. He pushed it out of his mind. Now was about more important things. Somehow, someway, they would find his dad and, together, they would find their way home.

Watch out for the return of Fyn Carter!

Acknowledgements

I've taken an age to write this book and there are many people to thank for their part.

To my family and friends: You've seen me through this long journey. Thank you so much. I've appreciated it every single time you've checked in and asked how the story was going. When I said I was going to write a book (series!) I know a few of you were surprised, but you've shown so much faith in me (even when I had doubts) and I'm grateful to you.

To the writing community: I'm now lucky enough to call many of you my friends. I've found my tribe and you're amazing. Thank you to those who were part of the Solent Fictioneers when I was finding my voice. Thank you to my Golden Egg classmates, to my fellow Write Magic sprinters, and to the Pitchford Writers. You are all creators of wonder, and I am awed by you.

I've been lucky enough to take on words of wisdom from some exceptionally wonderful and talented people within the writing industry. Thank you all, and in particular to Imogen Cooper, Adamma Okonkwo, Leonie Lock, Teara Newell, Annaliese Avery, Jenny Moore, Caroline Serpell, Cat Frankcom, and Chris Modafferi. In a vast multiverse of writers and editors, how amazing to have you all in my life on this version of Earth?!

Taking my time to write the story means many people got a sneak peek. Thank you to all of those who read early chapters and provided feedback: Alice Webster, Andy Mackay, Anne Wallis, Carina Buckley, Cass Elliott, Cat Frankcom, Debbie King, Ella Bolstridge, Fotis Mystakopoulis, Janet Gibson, Josh Lingard-Smith, Judith Hanley, Sarah Cotton, Sonia Sood, and Tom Crowhurst.

An extra big thank you to those who read an early version of the whole thing: Evelyn Edghill, Ian Luther, June Ross, Kay Richards, Luisa Belton-Lang, the Parris family (Frances, Neil, Zoe, and James), Richard Hunter, Steve Maidment, and Susan Streets.

Other mentions also go to: Alison Thayer, Carolyn Nicholson, the Carpenter family (Gabrielle, Mike, Joe, and Katie), Charlotte Cooper, Chrissy Sturt, the Hughes family (Tove, Maya, and Alex), Jo and Elliott Webster, Kiera Nixon, Lynden Wade, Rachel Lawston, Ruben Belton-Lang, Sam Gale, Simone Greenwood, Stuart White, and Vikki Marshall.

Thank you to Princess Jodie of Fairyham, who offered to read this book in its early stages but was unable to. Please feel free to read it over my shoulder xoxo

Thank you, Mum. Whatever project I'm working on, I know you are full of support, and it means so much. Of course I'll sign a copy!

Thank you, Dad. You say it how it is, and I'm so glad you're onside with this. I love the way you said you always thought I'd be a writer – even though you didn't tell me that until I worked it out for myself! :-)

Thank you to Ginny and Luna – my furbabies and writing mascots. If there's a notebook and a pen out or a video call happening, you can be sure there's a cat nearby. I'm furever grateful for your snugs.

A HUGE THANKS to Ian Luther, who has stood by me throughout this process and listened to me nattering away about Fyn and co. pretty much every single day for the last bunch of years. I owe you a great many cups of tea!!

Last but not least, thank you to everyone who reads and supports this book. I truly hope you love Fyn's first adventure as much as I've enjoyed creating it! If you do, please feel free to spread the word – reviews welcome! (",) Thank you Xx

Ian Hunter

Ian Hunter is a children's author who lives on the south coast of England, UK, with his partner and their two cheeky cats (aka writing mascots).

He loves anything creative and can usually be found writing, planning an adventure holiday, or escaping to a fantasy world.

Fyn Carter and the Agents of Eromlos is Ian's debut novel. He has many more stories to tell and is excited to share them with children and young-hearted adults like him everywhere.

Printed in Great Britain
by Amazon